*From the videotaped
last will and testament of
Max McKendrick*

Patience, honey, I've always felt responsible for your broken engagement to Alec Vaughn. If it wasn't for me you might've had a happy marriage and a whole passel of kids by now.

Therefore, to you, my only niece, I leave the entire Silver Spur Ranch horse-breeding business along with the log cabin home situated on its grounds. Naturally, you'll need a veterinarian to help you run things, so you might as well marry the fella and bring more than baby horses to life, if you catch my meaning. That being the case, I'm deeding Dr. Josh Colter half-interest in the whole operation. Refuse and your fifty-percent share of the business, with the exception of the cabin, will go to Josh. Either way, the two of you will be together forever.

Dear Reader,

The Silver Spur Ranch has a quarter of a million acres, but even it isn't big enough for the three McKendrick siblings and the intended spouses their uncle Max has bequeathed them. No place really is!

Once Max gives them the ultimatum—marry the mate he's chosen for them within forty-eight hours or lose their inheritance—it's a virtual stampede!

Join Cathy Gillen Thacker as she brings you all the sexy cowboys and wacky weddings you'd expect from WILD WEST WEDDINGS!

Don't miss any of the three WILD WEST WEDDINGS titles. The West was never like this!

Debra Matteucci
Senior Editor & Editorial Coordinator
Harlequin Books
300 East 42nd Street
New York, New York 10017

Cathy Gillen Thacker

THE RANCH STUD

Harlequin Books

TORONTO • NEW YORK • LONDON
AMSTERDAM • PARIS • SYDNEY • HAMBURG
STOCKHOLM • ATHENS • TOKYO • MILAN
MADRID • WARSAW • BUDAPEST • AUCKLAND

ISBN 0-373-16629-X

THE RANCH STUD

Prologue

Dear Patience,
The older I get, the more I see my options dwindling. So...do you believe an arranged marriage can be as successful as the more traditional counterpart?

Sincerely,
Desperately Seeking a Mate

Dear Desperately Seeking a Mate,
Only if the bride and groom do the arranging. Contrary to popular wisdom, arranged marriages never work! Hang tough and shoot for the whole ball of wax, not just an itty-bitty part.

Looking for True Love, Too,
Patience

"Are you all right?" thirty-eight-year-old Trace McKendrick asked his younger sister as he parked in front of the Silver Spur Ranch horse-breeding complex. It had been just twenty minutes since the reading of their beloved Uncle Max's will, and both were not only reeling with grief over their loss but stunned speechless by the highly unusual terms of their eccentric uncle's bequests.

"I could ask the same question of you," Patience McKendrick replied. She'd thought by now that she'd heard just about everything, but even ten years of writing an advice column to the lovelorn, peppered with stalwart western homilies, had not prepared her for this.

Trace shook his head. "I can't believe Uncle Max did this to us."

Patience reached over, squeezed his arm and commiserated grimly. "Tied all three of our inheritances to these incredibly foolish, hopelessly romantic—"

"Not to mention ill-advised—" Trace added with a discerning lift of his wheat blond brow.

"Unions!" Patience concluded emotionally.

"And, to top it all off, added a stipulation that we must marry within forty-eight hours or lose everything."

Patience sighed, ran a hand through her shoulder-length hair, the same shade as her brother's, and tried her best to look on the bright side. "I suppose it could be worse," she murmured finally as she smoothed the circle skirt of her long denim dress. Though she wasn't sure how.

Trace rolled his eyes, his displeasure unabated. "Yeah, we could be in little brother Cody's shoes and be expected to marry a woman Uncle Max had hand-picked from his Western Ranch Wives video match-making service, a woman who, as far as we can tell, Uncle Max had never even met!"

In Patience's view, she wasn't much better off than her younger brother, Cody, though Max had selected someone he had met for her—the Silver Spur Ranch veterinarian, Josh Colter. Worse, Max expected Josh

Colter to help her make the baby she had been wanting for as far back as she could recall. Max hadn't made that particular demand on her two brothers or their prospective mates, she thought resentfully.

"I don't even know how long my intended has been working at the ranch."

"Two months, I think," Trace replied. "I haven't met him yet, but my secretary saw him in town and said he was extremely fine in the looks department, in that distinctly rough-hewn, Montana-cowboy way."

"Well, who cares what he looks like!" Patience fumed.

Trace grinned. "You say that now," he teased. "But once you lay eyes on him—"

"Once I lay eyes on him nothing!" Patience shot right back, successfully fighting a blush. "At least you know your intended, Trace," she declared. "Unlike me, who has never even laid eyes on the Silver Spur Ranch employee I've been paired with!"

"Just because Susannah and I were married for three short months seventeen years ago does not mean I know her," Trace shot right back, bristling at the idea he had it any easier than his two siblings. "But you're right," he told Patience. "You do have it worse than I do, in that you've never met this ranch stud Uncle Max has hooked you up with."

"Nor am I sure I want to know Josh Colter." Patience scowled at the stud barn in mounting apprehension and sighed. As much as she hated to go in to face him, she knew she had no choice. Like it or not, it was time to play the cards she had been dealt.

Chapter One

Dear Patience,
Did you ever meet someone once, just for a few minutes, and know he was the one for you, against all reason?

Sincerely,
Head Over Heels

Dear Head Over Heels,
Life is not a romance novel. Put your feet back on the ground. Get your head out of the clouds.

Practical to a Fault and Proud of It,
Patience

48:00 hours and counting...

Patience entered the stud barn like a gunslinger from the Old West. Her heart was racing and she would have liked nothing better than to put this off, but because of the terms of her Uncle Max's will, she had no choice but to proceed at the breakneck pace he had set for her and her two brothers.

The concrete-floored barn smelled of fresh air and pine-scented disinfectant as she stepped past the tack room, where two cowboys in jeans, boots and regulation Silver Spur Ranch shirts were gathering up a handful of reins each.

Seeing her, Rusty and Slim dropped what they were doing and came over to greet her, their faces sad but respectful as they swept off their hats and held them to their chests. "We're all real sorry to hear about Max . . . we all loved the old coot," Rusty said thickly, then shook his head in mute commiseration. "It happened so suddenly."

Slim nodded, his gaze as mournful as his co-worker's as he choked out awkwardly, "This morning at dawn, instead of holding a moment of silence for him, we all gave him a big *yahoo* and threw our hats in the air. You know what a zest for life he had. We figured he woulda wanted it that way."

Patience wiped her eyes. The grief of the men who had worked for Max for many years had jump-started her own. "Thanks, fellas. I know Max appreciated that—" Swallowing hard around the lump in her throat, she sent a wistful glance overhead, adding, "Wherever he is."

Again, Rusty and Slim nodded, their expressions sober but subdued. It was hard to tell which of the grizzled cowpokes, who had worked the Silver Spur Ranch for more than fifty years between them, was suddenly more tongue-tied. "Gosh, it's good to have you back," Slim spit out finally.

Rusty nodded and regarded her like a long-lost but favorite niece. "It sure is." He paused, then plunged on awkwardly, his gnarled, arthritic fingers still worrying the brim of his hat. "If there's anything at all we can do for you, you just let us know," he said firmly.

Though still reeling inwardly with grief, Patience felt better just knowing Max's men were still there to protect and watch over her. "Actually, there is," she retorted seriously, still wishing she could delay the inevitable indefinitely. "I'm looking for Doc Colter, the new ranch veterinarian."

The two men exchanged glances. "Last I saw him he was outside with Soaring Eagle, at the other end of the barn," Rusty said finally.

Patience nodded her thanks, bid Rusty and Slim a subdued adieu and continued on her way. She found Soaring Eagle—but not Doc Colter—supervising the unloading of a visiting mare from a horse trailer. In a long-sleeved, collarless sienna shirt and blue jeans, his long black hair braided in a single plait down his back, a necklace of the Blackfoot tribe around his neck, the forty-five-year-old Native American was just as calm and unflappable as she remembered him. He paused long enough to hand the mare over to one of his assistants, then gave her a hug. They commiserated briefly about their loss and how much they would miss Uncle Max, then drew apart, tears in their eyes. "Welcome back," Soaring Eagle said, regarding her stoically.

"Thanks. It's good to be here," Patience replied. And she meant it. It felt good coming home. "But I've got to find Doc Colter."

"He's in the birthing barn, checking on one of the mares."

Patience smiled. "Thanks." Promising to come back and catch up on all the ranch news later, when they weren't so busy, she hurried over to the adjacent stable, one of ten on the horse compound, and stepped inside. Late afternoon, most of the stalls were empty, the mares—pregnant and otherwise—still out to pasture for the day. Sunshine and fresh air swept the impeccably clean facility.

Patience rounded the corner. Her steps slowed as she caught her first glimpse of the man her Uncle Max was insisting she marry. Her first thought was that Josh Colter was more cowboy than veterinarian. His straight dark hair was parted on the side and in need of a barber's trim. The soft, silky strands just brushed the tops of his ears and covered the nape of his neck. His skin bore what looked to be a year-round suntan, his nose had apparently been broken, but not set, and thick, arched brows bore the scars of seemingly more than one barroom brawl, but the rugged contours of his face were scrupulously clean and closely shaven. His worn Levi's jeans snugly hugged his long, muscular legs. A snowy white western shirt, the sleeves rolled up to his elbows, made the most of his broad shoulders and powerful—make that very powerful—six-foot-two physique. Add to that his silver-gray eyes . . . Patience had always had a weakness for men with silver-gray eyes.

"Josh Colter?" She ignored the little hitch in her breath.

"Yeah." Steadfastly ignoring the way she was scrutinizing him, he continued preparing a vitamin injection for a beautiful, mahogany, quarter horse mare. "You must be Patience McKendrick, Max's niece. Right?"

Something about his low, sensual voice, which was distinctly western in accent and rough in timbre, swiftly had her tingling with reaction. "How did you know?"

She had never met him before, and yet there was something vaguely familiar about him. Something she felt she ought to be able to identify, but to her deep frustration couldn't.

To her irritation, the rugged-looking animal doctor barely spared her a glance as he opened the chest-high wooden door and stepped into the stall, syringe in hand. "Light hair, blue eyes. You walk in like you own the place. You have to be one of the McKendrick heirs." He shrugged as if it were of little consequence to him who she was, or even why she was there.

Nor, unlike the other hired hands she had run into, did he commiserate with her over Max's passing. And that not only hurt her on an emotional level, it infuriated Patience, too. Josh hadn't worked here long, but surely he could have said something. "Step in here and give me a hand with Mandy, would you?" he ordered gruffly.

Knowing he did not really need her help—the sleek and beautiful Mandy might be very pregnant, but she was as docile as could be under the soothing stroke of Josh's callused hand on her shoulders—Patience dug in her heels. Regardless of Max's stipulations, she was not going to let Josh Colter or anyone else boss her around. And her husband-to-be might as well know that now. She folded her arms in front of her defiantly. "Sorry. Can't. I'm in my good clothes." She wasn't messing up her designer denim dress and silver concho belt for anything.

His lips curved into a goading smile that had her noticing another scar, a half-moon on the center of his lower lip.

"Trust me," Josh Colter drawled as he spared her a glance that made her heart race all the more. "Mandy here won't mind what you're wearing."

"That aside, I did not come down here to lend a hand," Patience said archly. In fact, she decided firmly, the farther she stayed away from a heartbreaker—with drop-dead gorgeous looks like his, he couldn't be anything but—like Josh Colter, the better, if she wanted to get out of the next forty-eight hours with her heart intact.

Josh sighed as he expertly gave the injection, then recapped and pocketed the empty syringe. "That, I probably should have guessed." Stepping behind the horse, he wordlessly checked the pregnant mare's drooping belly, then seemed to frown at what he either found or didn't see.

"What's the matter?" Patience asked anxiously, abruptly realizing she might have misjudged Josh after all.

Josh straightened and yanked off his surgical gloves. Gesturing at the feed bucket of warm bran mash laced with carrots outside Mandy's stall, he said, "That's what I'm trying to find out. According to Soaring Eagle, Mandy's been off her feed for several days now, and at this stage of her gestation, that's not good."

Patience handed over the bucket and watched as Josh softly coaxed Mandy to eat her feed. It was clear the horse was not the least bit hungry. Nevertheless, after another minute of determined coaxing on Josh's part, Mandy finally ducked her head and nibbled reluctantly at her specially prepared food. "You weren't kidding," Patience murmured after a moment, shocked at how little the mare was eating of the specially prepared meal. "You really are concerned about her, aren't you?" And now, so was Patience.

Josh shot Patience a brief glance, but it was long enough for her to get a full dose of his penetrating silver-gray gaze.

His sensual lips curved into the kind of half grin that indicated there wasn't much in this life that he took at all seriously. "Max was right. You are suspicious."

Patience felt her spine stiffen at the censure in Josh's low tone. She folded her arms in front of her defiantly. "Yes, well, I have good reason to be."

He blew out a dissenting breath. "I imagine that's debatable," he observed dryly, "but we'll get into that later." Reassured that Mandy was at least eating something, he gave the shiny-coated mare a final pat and stepped out of the stall.

"What do you mean, 'we'll get into that later'?" Patience parroted as she watched him close and latch the stall door. She made no effort to hide her annoyance.

"Apparently, Cisco Kidd left a message for me a little while ago. He said you would be wanting to talk to me, and soon, about the business of running this place." He was beginning to sound a little irritated himself as he strode toward the surgically clean washroom located in the center of the barn. "But since your Uncle Max, and not you, owns this operation, I can't imagine what you and I have to discuss on that front."

Patience paused, aware Josh's information on that fact was grievously wrong. Her breath caught in her chest as she inhaled the tantalizing scent of his cologne, recognizing it as English Leather. "Then you don't know . . ."

Josh blinked. "About what?"

"The will."

Josh's glance covered her from head to toe. He looked, if possible, even more irritated as he turned on the water and reached for the soap. Swiftly, he lathered his hands and scrubbed his muscular forearms until they were covered with silky white bubbles. "Whose will?"

"My Uncle Max's. It was read today."

Abruptly, Josh Colter stopped washing up and gazed at her uncomprehendingly. "You're telling me Max is dead?'' he repeated in a low, strangled voice, looking both incredibly grief-stricken and astonished.

Patience nodded slowly, sharing Josh's disbelief over her late uncle's demise. She knew exactly how Josh felt. She had felt the same way when she received the news. It seemed impossible Max was gone. He had always been so vital and full of energy, always making plans to carry out some new business venture or other, and he had always been so damned healthy. "He died a couple days ago, in town," she told Josh quietly. She and her brothers had only had enough time to show up for the private family memorial service and will reading.

She edged closer, curious now. "You're telling me you didn't know?"

Josh shrugged, as if he were still trying to make sense of what she'd told him. "I was away for a few days, checking out the soundness of some stallions and a few brood mares Max and I were thinking of acquiring for the ranch. I just got back from Wyoming half an hour ago. I showered, shaved, picked up a stack of messages I haven't had time to go through and came straight here to see how Mandy was doing." Genuine grief crossed Josh's face as he slowly turned to the sink and finished rinsing the soap from his arms. "No one told me about Max. But then I didn't talk to anyone, even Soaring Eagle, at length."

Patience couldn't say why exactly but it helped somehow, knowing Josh grieved as deeply for Max as she did. "Perhaps everyone assumed you already knew," she theorized quietly.

Josh nodded, accepting that explanation, as he tossed the soiled towel in the laundry bin. His expression grim, he swung around to face her. "How did it happen?"

Ignoring the mesmerizing depths of his gray eyes, Patience focused on the uncompromising way he had braced his shoulders against the wall. "Cisco said it was his heart, that it simply gave out on him."

"Where did it happen?"

"In Cisco Kidd's law office." Patience swallowed around the knot of emotion in her throat, and because Josh seemed as hungry for details as she had been, she tersely related what she knew. "Max had gone there to work on his will. He videotaped everything, so there'd be no question that these wishes were his later, and apparently the strain of doing it all at once was too much for him. For no sooner than he had completed it, he—" Tears filling her eyes, Patience flailed around looking for the right words and finally settled on a gentle western phrase she knew would have satisfied and amused Max. "He left us with his boots on, so to speak."

Josh was silent a long moment, reflecting, Patience guessed, on the unfairness of fate. "Couldn't the paramedics do anything?" he asked finally, his frustration evident.

Patience shook her head sadly. "It was over in a flash, before they even arrived, Cisco said. Which was as Max would've wanted it to be." He had always lived life on the edge. He would have wanted his death to be the same way, swift and sure, with no lingering, half-strength finales, Patience knew. Max could never have survived for long in an invalid's bed. He was an all-or-nothing type of person, just like Patience. And Cody. And Trace. And all the rest of the McKendrick clan.

His strides long and purposeful, Josh made his way back to Mandy's stall. Glancing over the door, he looked at the feed bucket and saw the quietly ailing mare had finished about a quarter of her evening feed but no more. "You took Cisco's word on that, I suppose?"

Sharing Josh's restlessness, Patience shoved her hands in the deep pockets of her dress. She paced back and forth, too, the soles of her soft suede boots making muted thuds on the concrete, the long skirt of her denim dress swirling femininely around her. "I've got no reason not to trust Cisco."

Josh smirked in response and made a rude, dissenting sound.

"Why do you not like Cisco?" Patience persisted, withdrawing both hands from her pockets. She was disturbed he would try to shake her faith in Max's attorney, who was also her old friend.

"Let's just say I can tell when someone is hiding something," Josh murmured enigmatically, his silver eyes narrowing. "And that guy has plenty of secrets. Speaking of which..." Josh let his voice trail off as he jerked his head toward the other end of the barn.

Patience turned and saw Cisco Kidd coming toward them. Though she hated to admit it, she knew exactly what Josh meant. She and her brothers had often wondered about Cisco's rather murky past, too.

Despite his tailored western business suits, fancy boots and trademark Stetson, Max's protégé had always been a little rough around the edges. Of course, that in itself was not necessarily a problem, Patience reminded herself sternly. In fact, Max had always admired Cisco Kidd's rough-and-tumble, from-the-streets quality and the way he had become sort of an adopted brother to Patience after her failed engagement, protecting her as fiercely as her real brothers, Cody and Trace. But there was no reason Josh Colter had to know the true nature of her relationship with Cisco, she thought, particularly if it would serve to keep them apart for the next forty-eight hours or so.

Patience smiled at her uncle's attorney and glanced at the package in Cisco's hand. "What have you got there?" she asked curiously.

At Patience's welcoming manner, Cisco seemed to relax. "It's the third part of Max's will."

Aware he was watching them both curiously, Patience turned to Josh and explained, "My brothers and I already heard the first videotape an hour ago in the Fort Benton Gentlemen's Club." And the first installment, which she had yet to relate to the unsuspecting Josh Colter, had been disturbing enough.

Patience turned back to Cisco with trepidation, hoping for a clue as to its contents. "I didn't know there was another part."

His expression serenely matter-of-fact, Cisco handed over a videotape marked Last Will And Testament Of Max McKendrick, Part Three. "This tape is just for you and Josh."

That didn't necessarily bode well, Patience thought, recalling the depth of her Uncle Max's eccentricity. In fact, it probably meant she should be even more on edge. "What about part two?" Patience asked impatiently.

"That was for Cody. Part four is for Trace."

"Oh."

"I suggest you both listen to that immediately," Cisco continued, indicating the videotape. He motioned Patience aside. Once out of the earshot of Josh, Cisco continued, "Regardless of how you and I feel about Josh, Max liked him a lot. He really took him under his wing. And, I think you should know, the two of them talked about you a lot.''

Patience felt a shiver of uneasiness ghost down her spine. ''What are you trying to tell me, Cisco?'' She paused, and when no immediate reply was forthcoming, she plunged on curiously. ''Are you trying to tell me you don't trust him?''

Cisco shot another wary look at Josh. ''I don't know what to think about him, Patience. I don't really know him well enough to decide if I should trust him or not. But Max did. And as you are about to discover for yourself, Max thought very highly of Josh. So you and I are going to have to go with Max's gut feeling on that. I just want you to be very careful.''

''You think he could hurt me, don't you?'' Patience probed, sensing there was something else going on here, too. Something else Cisco knew, or perhaps just suspected, but wasn't telling her.

Cisco shoved his hands in the pockets of his western-cut suit pants. ''I'm not saying Josh'd necessarily mean to, given how highly Max thought of him, but yeah, the possibility is there. So take care. And keep your eyes open. In the meantime, you've got my pager number, Patience, so you know how to get a hold of me if you need me.''

Patience nodded thoughtfully. ''That I do. Thanks, Cisco.''

Telling them he had another tape to deliver, Cisco said goodbye, then turned on his heel and left. Reluctantly, Patience turned back to Josh.

''What was all that whispering about?'' Josh demanded.

Patience shrugged. She was well used to all the men on the Silver Spur going overboard to watch out for her.

"Cisco is just trying to protect me," she replied matter-of-factly, not wanting to let her old friend's uneasiness get to her.

Josh grimaced as he ran his palm gently down the white blaze on the ailing Mandy's forehead. "Protect you or plant seeds of doubt?"

"Josh!" Patience reprimanded, shocked.

He shrugged his broad shoulders without a hint of apology and continued petting the mare. "It's an honest question. It deserves an honest answer."

That did it, Patience thought, still clutching the videotape. "He was trying to protect me," she repeated, feeling her temper start to rise at Josh's subtly provoking gaze, even as the woman in her appreciated the tenderness with which he was treating the mare. "After all, you haven't been around long, from what I understand. Just a couple of months. Cisco doesn't really know you."

"Nor am I sure the two of us want to get to know each other," Josh countered harshly, giving her a level look. "But that doesn't mean I am not a trustworthy person," he added as he dropped his hand and stepped away from Mandy.

His words struck a nerve. "No, of course it doesn't," Patience amended a little guiltily, lifting her glance to Josh's face. And in that instant, as he stepped toward her, as their eyes met and clashed, Patience was in for the shock of her life. For in Josh Colter's eyes, she swore she saw something more than just the similarity of color she had already noticed. She saw something . . . a hint of deeply ingrained gallantry or masculine possessiveness . . . that very much reminded her of Alec Vaughn, the only man she had ever loved, the man who had heartlessly jilted and humiliated her seventeen years ago.

"It can't be," Patience murmured emotionally, swaying unsteadily on her feet.

NOTING PATIENCE LOOKED as if she were going to faint at any second, Josh clamped a steadying arm around her waist. He'd thought maybe he'd overdone it at first, trying to show Max McKendrick's sassily independent niece precisely how much her electrifying presence did not affect him. But now that he actually had her in his arms, the playacting was over.

The impact of having her slender body so close to his was devastating. It had been years since he had been anywhere near her. During that time, so much had changed, and so little.

Her hair was still the same shimmering gold of a wheat field on a cloudless summer day. She wore it longer now, to her shoulders, where it tumbled in soft, loose, silky waves. Her long-lashed eyes were still a brilliant cornflower blue, her lips as full and soft. The curves on her tall, lithe body just as sweetly sensual. Holding her so close made it difficult to catch his breath.

And that in turn made Josh feel both uncomfortable and disloyal as hell. It was because of him that Patience had been suffering the way she had all these years. But sensing this was not the time, if ever there would be a time, to tell her that, he kept his secrets to himself. "What can't be?" he growled, struggling to keep a hold on his own mounting desire just to say to hell with his plan to rescue her from her own unhappiness and tell her everything now.

"You don't even look like him," Patience muttered, more to herself than him. "Alec was lanky and blond and bespectacled in that sort of sexy, bookish way. And you're so tall and dark and...and brawny, so you can't possibly—oh, dear heaven!" Patience stammered with a great deal more emotion than Josh cared to hear at that moment.

Their mutual problems were difficult enough without her turning all trembling and weak and needy on him. Or looking up at him with those vulnerable eyes. Eyes that he remembered so well. Eyes that had haunted his dreams.

"I hate to tell you this," Josh shot back gruffly, working to keep his own emotions at bay as he tore his eyes from the soft, sensual contours of her full lips, "but you're not making any sense." At least she wouldn't be, he added mentally, if he didn't already know damn well what she was talking about.

Patience passed a hand over her brow in the age-old signal of a female in distress and clung to him all the more. "Tell me about it," she moaned, wrapping her arms around him tightly.

"Maybe you'd better sit down." Josh swept her off her feet and up into his arms, carried her back to the washroom, set her down in the lone straight-backed chair in the room and leaned over her to look her in the face. "You okay?"

Patches of pink were now highlighting the ivory color of her skin.

"Fine. It's just..." Patience balled her hands into fists and shook herself slightly. Her teeth raked her soft lower lip. "I guess it's been a stressful couple of days."

He waited for her to go on. To both his relief and his disappointment, she didn't. "I'm sorry," Josh said, finally figuring it had to be the grief that was making her act so crazy. At least they could blame it on that later, if the subject of her almost recognizing him ever came up. "Your Uncle Max was a great man," he said sincerely, meaning it from the bottom of his heart.

Patience nodded. Looking abruptly afraid her grief would get the better of her again, she brushed a hand through her hair and said, "Shall we listen to the videotape?"

Josh nodded. Maybe that was a good idea. "Right away."

TOGETHER, THEY WALKED over to Josh's office. To her relief, Patience was feeling much better by the time Josh had settled her in one of the thick leather chairs, got her a cold drink to help revive her and put the tape into the machine they kept around to show horse buyers videotapes on the farm practices and procedures.

To her trepidation, part three of Uncle Max's videotaped will began much as part one had. Her Uncle Max, clad in his trademark fringed buckskin jacket, mustard yellow chaps and silver spurs, appeared on the screen. As before, there was no sign of his impending departure from this world. His skin was a deep, leathery tan beneath his long, Lone Star mustache, his white, shoulder-length hair thick and shiny clean. Though he was nearly as old as the hills when the tape was made, he was still as energetic as the day was long.

On-screen, Max began to speak. "Hello, Patience and Josh. I imagine you've had your first meeting by now, which was—unless I miss my guess—as full of sparks as a sparkler on the Fourth of July."

"I wouldn't exactly put it that way," Patience mumbled, still feeling embarrassed about the way she had first quarreled with Josh, then nearly fainted in his arms.

"Max would," Josh murmured back, tongue in cheek.

"And you're probably anxious for me to quit jawin' and cut to the chase, but before I get started, I've got something of a personal nature to say. Patience, I think you know that for a long time now, I have blamed myself for your situation. Many a time I've thought if I had just agreed to go to your wedding to Alec Vaughn, you would already be happily married and bringing up a passel of kids. And the fact you never got seriously involved with another fella after your broken engagement sort of intensified that feeling on my part."

Patience blushed fire-engine red, knowing everything Max had just said was true.

"So a couple of months ago, I called in all my markers with a few of my World War II buddies, who, though retired now, still have ties in the intelligence community. And I asked them to find out what they could for me." Max paused, his expression becoming abruptly mournful. "I'm sorry to say Alec Vaughn died of complications from pneumonia, about five years after he jilted you, in his native state of Louisiana."

While tears started in Patience's eyes, Max shook his head sadly. "I had hoped for a better outcome to my search. Still," he went on firmly, "it's better to know one way or another." He paused, all the love he had ever felt for Patience reflected in his blue eyes. "I hope this closes the circle for you and enables you to go on with your life. I always have and always will want only the best for you."

Josh touched her arm. To Patience's surprise, Josh looked as shocked and upset by what Max had just disclosed to them via videotape as she felt. "You okay?" Josh whispered.

Patience nodded. With a little help from Max in heaven above, she would be.

"Anyway," Max continued soberly, "it's time to get back to the business of sorting out my legacy. So here's the deal...." He energetically slapped his buckskin-clad knee before going on.

"Patience, honey, I know you want a baby more than anything in the world, and I want that for you, too. But if you're going to do somethin' like this, you need to do it right, and that starts by picking out a fine daddy to sire your child. Josh Colter is such a man. In fact, I think you two would make a fine pair. Which is why I am leaving Patience the log cabin home, complete with writing studio, along with the substantial parcel of land the horse-breeding business is situated on. Naturally, you'll need a veterinarian to help you run things, and that being the case, as I said in my previous videotape, you might as well marry the fella and bring more than baby horses to life, if you catch my meaning. As I said before, he's handsome and smart and willing—"

"I never said any such thing! The two of us only talked about me running the ranch!" Josh interrupted heatedly. He turned to Patience, incensed. "In fact, the subject of me being your stud, Patience McKendrick, was never even broached!"

He didn't have to act so opposed to it! Patience glared at Josh and clapped a hand across her chest. "Like I requested you? For heaven's sake, we never even met! To think that I—we—" She blushed and couldn't go on.

"You'll also need someplace bigger to raise that passel of kids you've always wanted, so Lost Canyon is yours, too. I've set aside money for you to build a dream home there. If you get started on it right away, it'll be finished by the time that first baby of yours is born.''

On-screen, Max continued with the down-home affability for which he was famous. ''Naturally, Josh will want to get something out of this besides a new boss and a baby, so I am deeding him half interest in the horse-breeding business.'' Max's expression became more sober. ''I don't imagine this will sit too well with you, Patience, having a man underfoot after all these years of you being more or less on your own, so I put a few conditions on this inheritance of mine.''

''Of course,'' Patience murmured.

''Should you refuse to marry Josh, you will lose all rights to the land, your fifty percent share of the horse business, your rights to Lost Canyon and the funds to build your dream house, maintaining only the log cabin home containing your writing studio—which is, of course, located right next to the horse-breeding ranch complex.

''Should Josh refuse to marry you, he will get nothing from my estate. I don't think that will happen, mind you. Josh is a smart fella. He knows if he just sticks with my plan, he will be set for life, with a great job and a great place to live. And what are forty-eight hours and a wedding, after all?''

''In this case, an eternity,'' Patience muttered.

''I'll second that,'' Josh added as the videotape continued.

Max smiled warmly at them both from the screen.

''Either way, you two will be stuck together forever and ever, living and working side by side as long as you remain on this ranch. So you might as well make the best of it. Meantime, I'll see you at the wedding forty-eight hours from now." He lifted a cautioning hand. "Meantime, although the two of you are free to roam wherever you want or need to go, I expect the two of you to stay together under the same roof twenty-four hours a day, with no more than three thirty-minute separations. You break the rules and the deal is off. I don't imagine you will like that much, either."

"No more than I like anything else," Patience muttered.

"You can second me on that sentiment, too," Josh added grimly.

"But I want you two young'uns to listen up and listen good anyway," Max continued, as if lecturing a wayward child. "When you go to a dance, the proper thing to do is to dance with the one that brung you. That applies here, too. So no more mooning over your lost love, Alec Vaughn, Patience McKendrick. 'Cause you know now for certain what I think we have all long sensed, that he's never coming back to you. And, Josh, no more moving on every time a new wind blows. It's way past time you both made a fresh and lasting start for yourselves."

"As if it were just that easy," Patience said, perturbed.

"It might be," Josh replied with an unnervingly pensive look in her direction, "given that the time and the woman and the moment were right. Which is not to say that this is the case here and now," he added sarcastically.

"Amen to that," Patience shot right back.

Oblivious to the tension in the room, which was so thick it could have been cut with a knife, Max continued on-screen, "I know you both probably have a ton of questions. Cisco Kidd can answer a lot of them, especially the ones that pertain to the terms of the will and the triple wedding I set up for all three of my heirs. As for the rest, I'd advise you to just listen to your hearts. 'Cause if you do, I guarantee you'll know what to do.''

Max tipped his hat at them. "Happy trails. Remember I love you," he said huskily, "and know I'll always be thinking of you."

At the sentiment in her uncle's low voice, Patience's heart ached and her eyes flooded with tears. Uncle Max's picture faded to an endless vista of blue Montana sky, then to black.

JOSH GOT UP to turn off the television and videotape machine. "I knew your uncle was eccentric, but—"

"It's a lot to take in, isn't it," Patience admitted with a weary shake of her head. First losing Max, then all hope of ever seeing Alec Vaughn again.

He edged closer. "Who is this Alec Vaughn, anyway?"

Patience shook her head. This was the umpteenth time Alec's name had come up today, which was, undoubtedly, why she had thought she had seen Alec in Josh, when the reality was that no two men could have been more different. Alec was gone forever, she knew that now; Josh was still here. Alec had been sweet, blond, with an incredibly sensitive and poetic soul. Josh—though drop-dead gorgeous in his own way—was brawny and rough-hewn to a fault. Alec had been classically handsome, his nose arrow straight. Josh's face was scarred, his nose broken, at least once if she had to guess. Alec had been thin and tall in that wiry, nonjock way. Josh was also tall but he was muscled from head to toe, his shoulders twice as wide. The only resemblance the two men had was the color of their eyes, which were a seductive silver-gray. But even there, there were differences. Alec's eyes had been loving, warm, open. Josh's eyes were cynical, challenging, untrusting in the extreme. "It's not important," she said at last.

Josh studied her. To her chagrin, he was unwilling to let it go. "Max seemed to think it was. He seemed to think you were still in love with him after all this time."

Patience set her chin. "Max was wrong. I gave up on the idea of ever having a life with Alec again a long time ago."

Josh lifted a skeptical brow. "Was Max wrong about your wanting a baby, too?"

"No," Patience allowed plainly. She looked into Josh's eyes and knew she had been crazy to see Alec in him, even for a minute. The two men were as different as night and day. The way Josh kept pushing her was proof of that. "That much is right on target. I do want a baby." Desperately.

"I see." Josh snorted derisively. "You just don't much care who the father is."

For some reason, Patience noted, this notion bothered Josh Colter. It bothered him a lot. Though she didn't see why it should. It was none of his business who fathered her future child—or children. She shrugged her slender shoulders, admitting, "So I've given up on finding the perfect mate." *So what? It wasn't as if Josh were married or the least bit settled, either!*

Josh quirked a disapproving brow. "I gather your two siblings have given up on finding the perfect mates, too?"

"My brothers have been as unlucky in love as I have."

"And yet you're considering Max's demands, aren't you?" This stunned him.

Patience sighed and explained, "We all are going to do our best to see Max's wishes are carried out. It's the least we can do after all he did for us."

"Which was—?"

Her voice softened. "He took us in when our parents died." Years later he had done the same for his protégé, Cisco Kidd. "He gave up a lot to raise us. Without Max, we probably all would have ended up in foster homes."

"And yet none of you are married?" Josh concluded heavily.

Patience cringed. "According to Max, that was his fault as much as ours. Early on, he was a bit too involved in our love lives," she added wryly.

Again, Josh looked surprised. He sat back down and took a sip of the soft drink he'd got for himself. "How so?"

"He loaned Trace the money to start his own business as a wedding gift. Trace was so busy proving himself he didn't have any time for Susannah and she split. He encouraged Cody to elope with Callie Sheridan, who was seven years his junior. It was too soon, I guess, because Callie ran out on Cody during their honeymoon and Cody has yet to get over it." In fact, he had been living like a hermit. He hadn't had a haircut or a shave in ages. . . .

"And you?"

There was no other way to put it. "I was jilted on my wedding day."

"By this Alec Vaughn guy," Josh guessed slowly.

"Yes."

Josh shook his head. His silver eyes were reflective. Abruptly, he seemed a million miles away as he murmured, "You must hate the guy, then."

"Not really," Patience allowed, knowing her anger with Alec had long disappeared. She continued with earnest intensity, "If not for Max—" Her mouth tightened in a mutinous line.

"What?" Josh rested a forearm on his thigh and leaned forward in his chair.

Patience studied the toes of Josh's handcrafted western boots. "You heard what Max said on the tape. Max didn't want us to marry. He told Alec if he insisted on going through with the wedding he would have no choice but to disinherit me."

"And so your fiancé skipped out on the ceremony," Josh concluded grimly.

"He left town altogether. Never to be heard of again, at least not by anyone the two of us knew at Yale."

"And you blame Max for that?" Josh regarded her incredulously.

Patience knew she had good reasons for feeling that way. She got up to throw her empty soft drink can in the recycling bin. "I'm sure Alec was only trying to do what was best for both of us, leaving that way. I'm sure he was only trying to protect me." Because Alec had loved her—she knew it! There was no faking the way they had felt, no faking the passionate love she had seen reflected in his eyes.

Josh drained the rest of his drink in a single gulp, then crushed the empty can in his hands. He regarded her boldly, making no effort to mask the icy cynicism in his gaze. "Then again, maybe he was just after your—or more specifically, Max's—money. Maybe he split when he saw he wasn't going to get any. Maybe you're better off without him.''

Patience had heard the same spiel many times. From Max, her brothers, even Pearl, the proprietress of Pearl's Diner in Fort Benton. She watched as Josh got up to throw the can into the bin beside hers.

"You don't know anything about Alec!" Patience replied indignantly, sure she had been right about this much. "Alec was a sensitive, caring—"

"Fool?" Josh interjected politely.

Patience clamped her arms together in front of her. She knew there was some reason she did not like Josh. As it turned out, he was much too judgmental. "I am not going to discuss him with you," she announced, only wishing she had made that decision sooner.

Josh regarded her gravely, as if he had already expected as much. "It probably helps soothe your wounded pride, doesn't it, canonizing your ex-fiancé this way. But it doesn't help anything else."

Patience glared at him. She had already heard the same from her brothers, from Cisco, from Uncle Max. She did not want to hear it from Josh Colter, too. "Are you finished?"

Her tone was enough to freeze the fires of hell, but to her growing annoyance, he merely ignored her. Crossing to his desk, he picked up a bone-colored Stetson and fitted it on his head, pulling it low across his brow to shield his eyes.

Ignoring her increasingly forbidding look, he continued lazily, "I can also see why Max wanted me involved here. I've certainly got my work cut out for me."

Patience stomped closer, planted both her hands on her hips and regarded Josh as she would a rival boxer stepping into the ring. "Let's get something perfectly clear here, Dr. Colter. I loved my uncle dearly, despite his flaws when it came to parenting three very willful and energetic adolescent kids. And mine in behaving with nothing even resembling childlike obedience. So, in an effort to honor my Uncle Max, I will do my best to carry out his last wishes and stick to your side like glue for the next forty-eight hours. I will write my column in the writing studio he built for me and live under the same roof as you and accompany you on whatever it is you do around here. And I will even willingly take part in the triple wedding he set up for Trace, Cody and myself and our appointed mates. But that is absolutely as far as I am going,'' Patience announced determinedly.

Half of Josh's mouth lifted in a knowing curl. And she knew even before he uttered one syllable that she was not going to like what he said. "No baby making?'' he asked guilelessly.

Irritated beyond belief, Patience tossed her head. Her blond hair flew away from her face in silky waves. "You better believe there is going to be no baby making.''

Josh's eyes twinkled with devilish lights as they caressed first the tousled layers of her hair and then her upturned face. "How about just getting married, then,'' he propositioned boldly, as if unable to resist, "and saving the baby making for a more appropriate date.''

That was another difference between Josh and Alec, Patience thought. Alec didn't tease, especially about things that were this important!

"There is no way I am trapping a man—any man!— into a lifetime marriage, even a rude, reckless cowboy like you,'' she replied.

Again, Josh Colter favored her with that goading half smile. With the tip of one finger, he pushed the brim of his hat back until it sat at a rakish angle, then tilted his ruggedly handsome face down to hers. "And why not, *ma'am?*"

He put heavy emphasis on the last word—just to annoy her, Patience was sure. His ploy worked.

With effort she controlled her temper and confronted him as bluntly and honestly as she knew how. "Because there's no better way to ensure a marriage will fail than to force someone to the altar. And," she continued with unabashed chagrin, "it's no secret around here that I have already failed once at this getting-married business. I have no intention of doing it again. So..." She fastened her eyes on Josh's, figuring they might as well lay all their cards on the table now. "Will you help me or not?" she said.

Chapter Two

Dear Patience,
Should I marry for reasons other than love?
                                        Signed,
                        Not Getting Any Younger

Dear Not Getting Any Younger,
That's like asking if you should buy a horse that's
half-sound. Shoot for the whole package, honey.
                        You Won't Be Disappointed,
                                        Patience

In the past, Josh had considered himself remarkably
laid-back and easygoing. But these days, due largely to
a more or less ongoing devastating personal experience
that he did not want to share with Patience Mc-
Kendrick or anyone else on the Silver Spur, he did not
take kindly to people who used or coerced others to
achieve their own means. And that included the incredibly beautiful woman in front of him.

"That all depends," Josh drawled, towering over her
in a way that he knew darn well would intimidate her.
"What's in it for me?"

Patience McKendrick tensed at the edge in his voice, as he knew she would, but she defiantly kept her ocean blue eyes locked on his. "A generous cash settlement after we divorce."

As if that were all it would take to get him enmeshed in the late Max McKendrick's baby-making strategy. "Which will be when?" Josh countered, figuring he already knew the answer to that.

"Just as soon as Cisco Kidd, Uncle Max's attorney, says it is okay."

Though he was tempted to acquiesce solely for the pleasure of having Patience in his bed—where she soon would be if she was his wife, Josh couldn't help but think—he was not about to let Patience or Max or anyone else in her eccentric family use him like so many bundles of money to get what they wanted, no matter how guilty he felt about what had happened to her in the Alec Vaughn matter. Sure, now it was easy to see how the whole catastrophe could have been avoided— and Alec's life, such as it was then, spared—if only he had been paying more attention to everything that was going on around him. But he hadn't been, Josh admitted, because then, all he'd been able to think about was his own future and that of the woman he had loved and subsequently lost. Aware Patience was waiting for an answer from him, Josh frowned. "No deal," he said shortly, turning down her offer of a buyout point-blank.

Patience blinked, apparently unprepared for his refusal. "Don't you want what Max left you?" she asked, stunned.

Considering the chain of events that had led him to the nomadic life of a wanderer and then the Silver Spur, Josh didn't even have to think about it. "Not at that

price,'' he said. He might not be honest about everything these days, but in those areas where he could be,
he was scrupulously truthful and forthright. He wasn't
marrying Patience McKendrick, only to divorce her.
When he married, *if* he married, it was going to be for
life.

"Then what price will it take?" Patience persisted,
still intently watching his face.

Aware they had been standing too close for too long,
Josh moved away from her once again, finally seating
himself on the edge of his desk. "For starters, hordes
of money does not solve people's problems. I'd wager
it creates them." In fact, Josh had only to look back
into his own past, to the day he had found out how
money, and the desperate need and want of it, had im-
pacted his own life and all those close to him. . . .

*HE COULD STILL recall his shock as he stood in the
doorway, unable to believe what he saw. A member of
his own family not only associating with such scum but
actually doing business with them! Disgusted and dis-
illusioned at the sight of the money changing hands, he
was about to turn away, when the conversation abruptly
took on a vile tone.*

*His heart thudding heavily in his chest, he set his
backpack down carefully and listened to the thugs re-
peat their demand his family take part in the murder of
one of their neighbors and friends.*

*To his relief, the demand was refused outright. But
not, as expected, without a terrible price. Their expressions ugly and menacing, the thugs swiftly produced a
pair of brass knuckles and a heavy metal club.*

He didn't even have to think about what to do next. Unarmed and unprepared, he barreled in to the rescue....

And had regretted everything that had happened ever since.

"MEANING WHAT, EXACTLY?" Patience drawled, snapping him back to the present. Aware she was waiting for him to continue stating his position on Max's wishes, Josh concluded, "So I'm not interested in the inheritance." The horses on the ranch, however, were another matter. He was very much interested in them. Max had owned some beautiful stock. Josh had enjoyed taking care of them. "Two," Josh continued, figuring he might as well spell it all out now, "if and when I have a baby with a woman, I want it to be our decision. Not hers. Not mine."

Patience shrugged her slender shoulders. "I agree that would be the optimum situation. Unfortunately," she continued, sending a droll look in his direction that carried with it absolutely no invitation to partake in parenthood with her, "it doesn't always work out that way."

A cowboy could dream, couldn't he? "You'd be surprised what you can accomplish if you set your mind to it." Take his ending up on the Silver Spur. There were some—Holly Diehl included—who felt this was the last place on earth he should be. But Josh knew they were wrong. He knew that he owed it not just to Alec and himself but to Max, to make sure his niece was all right. Right now, despite Patience's feisty declarations to that effect, he was not sure that was the case.

"Listen, Josh, all I am talking about is us getting married, as briefly as possible, as per the terms of the will. Nothing else." Patience seated herself on the edge of his desk, too, so they were side by side, almost like two kids on the edge of a dock, fishing.

Not mollified in the least by her aggressively pragmatic attitude, Josh looked down at the way her slender fingers were curved on the wood and shook his head. "Again, I'm not interested," he said.

"Why not?" Patience shifted so their thighs were touching. She was plainly vexed.

Josh looked down into her upturned face. "Because with me it's all or nothing there, too," he retorted, letting her know with a glance that he was through living his life in halfway measures. And she should be, too, he thought. "If I were to agree to marry you, I would want it to be a real and binding arrangement, not some sham acquiescence to your Uncle Max's wishes. In short, I would want it all. You, the dream home in Lost Canyon, the horse-breeding operation and, yes, even the baby Max wanted us to have. If I were to agree, I would want it to be worth any time and energy we would put into the relationship."

Patience was as incensed as he expected her to be by the "grand scale" of his demands. "Well, that isn't even an option, Josh. The way things stand, you can't have it all! And neither can I."

"Fine. Then you're on your own," Josh retorted, knowing that was what Max would have wanted, too. Not waiting for her reply, he levered himself off the edge of the desk and headed for the door.

Patience hopped down and trotted after him. She wrapped her fingers around his forearm and tugged. "Josh, wait."

Josh looked down at her and tried not to think about what the feel of those delicate fingers against his bare skin was doing to him. Or how guilty he felt, realizing that he already knew the truth about what had really happened to Alec Vaughn and Patience didn't.

"Let's not be hasty," Patience continued.

Josh pried her fingers from his arm. "You're saying you'll change your mind?" Damn, but he wished things were simpler.

"No, I am saying," Patience clarified, clearly enunciating every word, "that I need forty-eight hours to think about it."

"And then what?" Josh demanded, resisting the urge to drag her into his arms and kiss some sense into her. Someone had to!

"Then," Patience said, "we'll see."

SILENCE FELL BETWEEN THEM.

Patience saw she'd bought herself time, but not much. Josh Colter was a man who would only tolerate being put on hold for a little while. But a little while was all it would take to grant Uncle Max's last wish ... and maybe by the time they had done that, Josh would realize the idea of their marrying, really marrying, was just too crazy to be borne, even if it was what Max had clearly wished.

"This has been a little sudden," Josh said finally.

"And then some." Able to see he was coming around, Patience sighed her relief.

"Maybe we should think about it," Josh suggested, his steady gaze still roving her upturned face.

Patience smiled in complete agreement. After all, thinking was not the same as doing. "Absolutely," she said cheerfully.

"While at the same time not permanently closing any doors," Josh continued.

"Right on."

Another silence. "In the meantime, do you feel up to taking a couple of horses out on the range?" Josh asked.

Patience didn't even have to think about that. A horseback ride at sunset on the Silver Spur sounded like exactly what she needed. "Sure." Patience nodded, glad Josh had suggested it. She looked down at her long denim dress. "I've got to change into jeans, though—"

"I want to check on Mandy one last time, see how she did with her feed. Unless you want to use one of our three thirty-minute time-outs now?" Josh said.

Reminded of the strict conditions surrounding her inheritance from Uncle Max, Patience shook her head. "No, we might need it more later."

"True."

They found Mandy had eaten all her bran mash. The gleaming mahogany quarter horse was standing quietly in the large birthing stall, her rump pressed up against the rear wall.

As Josh studied the mare, he talked to her softly, but she did not come forward to see him, as expected. "How far along is she?" Patience asked quietly.

Still murmuring soft words of encouragement to the mare, Josh opened the door latch on the twenty-by-twenty-foot stall and stepped inside. "She's in her three-hundred and twenty-ninth day of gestation."

"So she could foal anywhere from the next couple days through the next three weeks and still be in the normal range," Patience said. Which explained, she thought, why Josh was so attentive.

"Right." Josh stepped around to check Mandy out, then returned to Patience's side. Satisfied all was well for the moment, he scrubbed his arms to the elbow in a nearby sink. "You ever assisted in a foaling?"

"No. I've watched mares give birth but not for many years." Patience looked back at Mandy. Though quiet, she seemed pretty miserable. Her dark eyes were dull and listless, her overall posture one of fatigue. "Is she an experienced brood mare?"

Josh stroked his hand down the white blaze on Mandy's face. "No. This is her first time. So neither of us knows how it's going to go, but so far—except for being off her feed for the last week or so—she's been shaping up well. So we're keeping a close eye on her." He gave Mandy a final pat and reached for the phone on the wall outside the stall. He spoke to Soaring Eagle, giving him an update on Mandy's condition as well as a rundown on his own plans, then hung up the phone. His expression was matter-of-fact. "Soaring Eagle has the hands saddling up a couple of horses for us, so as soon as you're ready, we'll go."

"I THOUGHT memory and sentiment had exaggerated the beauty of the Silver Spur Ranch in early June. I was wrong. It's even more breathtaking than I recall," Patience told Josh as they reined in their horses atop the ridge overlooking what those on the ranch liked to refer to as Lost Canyon. Surrounded by granite-topped mountains on all four sides, the valley was lush and green, peppered with trees, a ribbonlike river running through the middle.

Josh nodded at the far corner of the canyon. "Keep watching."

A moment later, a band of wild mustangs shot across the far edge of the canyon. Ranging from dark brown to gray to solid white, they were without exception all fast and sleek. Watching them, Patience found herself smiling in delight. "How long have those been here?"

"A couple of years. At first there were only a few, but as you can see, their numbers are increasing."

"I count...ten?"

Josh continued to watch the mustangs race across the canyon. "And there are more."

"On McKendrick land?" Patience was surprised but pleased to discover this.

"Yes. They just showed up here recently."

She sat back in her saddle and lifted a cautioning brow. "You know they're a protected species?"

Josh nodded. "I've already gotten permission from the local authorities of the Bureau of Land Management to adopt any I can catch, tame and certify as healthy. But right now, as long as their numbers are manageable, as long as they're not bothering any ranch operations, I'd prefer to see them continue to run free, rather than imprison them unnecessarily."

"I know what you mean," Patience said, heartened to discover that she and Josh passionately agreed on something. "They are beautiful. I can't imagine a better life for them than being able to run free in such a spectacular place."

Josh nodded back at the canyon. "This is where Max said you wanted your dream home?"

"Once. A very long time ago." *When I was engaged to Alec.* Determinedly, Patience shook off her melancholy over the dreams she'd failed to achieve and concentrated instead on what was still within her grasp—*like having a baby.* Taking a deep breath, she continued informatively, "It's the perfect site for a home." *The perfect site to raise a family.*

Looking over at Josh, she couldn't help but note that he seemed to think so, too. In fact, he could hardly take his eyes off the place.

"If this was what you wanted, why didn't you build it anyway, on your own?" Josh asked as they rode slowly back, side by side.

Patience shrugged, unwilling to admit that she hadn't wanted just a home and a baby but a home with Alec and Alec's baby, and up until today, a very small but extremely determined part of her had been unconsciously holding out for just that. But now, with Alec gone, she knew her Uncle Max was right. She had to move on, even if she had to push herself a little to do so.

"I wasn't living here," Patience answered Josh adroitly.

"Why not? Ten to one, you could write that column of yours anywhere."

Patience's lips tightened into a mutinous line. Not since Alec had anyone asked her so many difficult questions, so fast. Patience trained her eyes on the horizon and wished her Uncle Max had not linked her to such a complicated man, even for a little while. "I stayed away for lots of reasons," she said finally.

"Chief among them your falling out with your uncle?"

"You heard about that," Patience ascertained, wishing he hadn't. It embarrassed her, in retrospect, because as she had matured she had realized there had been far better ways to handle that situation. And worse, precious time lost with Max, time that she knew now could never be regained.

Josh nodded, relaying casually, "The story around here is that the two of you went almost a year without exchanging even a single word."

Patience shrugged as her mount picked her way through a meadow peppered with wildflowers. "I was furious with him for interfering in my engagement to Alec." And she'd had reason to be. Uncle Max had behaved terribly, refusing even to meet Alec, once he'd learned of their wildly passionate love affair and hasty engagement.

"But you forgave Max eventually."

Patience made a seesawing motion with her hand. There were some things that were simply best forgotten, especially since this was something that was just never going to be remedied. "It was more like I agreed to overlook it. It's not quite the same thing."

Josh gave her an intent, sidelong look. "You're still carrying a torch for this guy, Vaughn?"

Patience wished she could say the reverse was true, but it wasn't. She knew there was always going to be a part of her heart that belonged to Alec.

Unwilling, however, to hear a lecture on the subject from even one more well-meaning person, she urged her mount forward, ahead of his, and snapped, "Whether I am or not, it's none of your business." Besides, it didn't matter. Alec was dead.

Josh spurred his horse on and caught up with her until they were even once again. "As the man you are trying to talk into marrying you in less than forty-eight hours—" he shouted to be heard, looking over at her face "—it is very much my business."

Patience shrugged and leaned forward defiantly in her saddle, urging her horse to go even faster. She supposed he had a point. It didn't mean, however, that she was going to change her mind. Ignoring him, she trained her eyes straight ahead, on the sun sinking slowly toward the horizon, and shouted right back,

"Whatever, your curiosity is not going to be satisfied, so you may as well give up."

LIKE HELL HE WOULD GIVE UP, Josh thought as they stopped a moment later to give their horses a much needed drink at a nearby stream.

"About the baby and the ranch," he began.

That caught her attention, just as he had hoped it would.

"Yes?" Patience demanded.

"I'm curious. If you wanted a child so much, and you're so all-fired determined to remain a very independent woman, why didn't you just have a child via one of the sperm banks in Denver and bring your baby back here to the ranch to raise?"

Color flooded her cheeks. "Because," Patience said stiffly as the last of the day's sunlight filtered down through the trees, catching the golden highlights in her soft, tousled hair.

"Because why?" Josh uncapped the canteen he'd brought with him and handed it to her.

Patience drank deeply of the cold water inside, then delicately blotted the dewy moisture on her lips with the back of her hand. "Because Max and I were not in agreement on the subject, that's why." Having had her fill, she handed the canteen to him.

"He thought having a baby via artificial insemination was unnatural?" Josh lifted the canteen to his lips and drank deeply, too.

"And unwise."

The taste of her, mingling with the taste of the water, lingered on his lips as Josh recapped the canteen. "But you liked the idea," he said.

"No. Not really." Patience sighed, a troubled light darkening her eyes to a stormy ocean blue. "I just didn't see I had any choice."

She was wrong about that, Josh thought. People always had more choices than they knew, if only they stopped to thoroughly consider all their options. For instance, if he had handled things better, "Alec Vaughn" might still be here.

He couldn't do anything about that now, of course. What was done was done. But he could act to assuage his own guilt in Alec's untimely disappearance and, with the help of Max McKendrick's eccentric will, ensure that Patience, too, put the past behind her and one day achieved the full family life she deserved.

"I told Uncle Max he was being hopelessly old-fashioned, thinking that I needed to be married to someone, in the forever-and-ever way, before I brought a child into this world," Patience continued. As their horses drank from the stream, she leaned against the trunk of a nearby tree.

Josh braced a hand on the trunk beside her. "And still no go?"

Patience's pretty chin jutted out stubbornly as she looked up at him. She folded her arms in front of her, tucking them just beneath her breasts. "I could have persuaded him, if I'd had more time," she declared.

Josh just bet she could have. One pleading look from her eyes had him feeling pretty helpless.

"On what basis?" Josh asked, warning himself that the last thing either of them needed was for him to be too susceptible to Patience McKendrick's considerable charms. Just because the blue-eyed blond spitfire was sexy as hell, just because she had curves in all the right places and long, luscious legs that wouldn't quit did not mean he had to fall prey to her spell.

"What's important is that I could give a child love and attention and all the tender loving care he could stand."

"But said child would still need a daddy," Josh pointed out, knowing there was a part of him that wanted nothing more than to volunteer for the job of taking Patience McKendrick to bed and siring their children.

"I know, and I had that covered, too," Patience continued.

He quirked a brow to let her know he was interested in whatever she was thinking.

"I've got two brothers who are both living here on the Silver Spur. And up until a couple of days ago, I had Uncle Max, too. If I'd had a baby here, all three could have stepped in and played daddy to my child, just as Uncle Max played mama and daddy to my brothers and I, after my parents died in that earthquake."

"So do it. Have your baby now," Josh advised.

Again, Patience sighed. "I can't."

Josh could feel her putting up roadblocks again. He wanted only to tear them down. "Why not?"

Patience dug the toe of her handcrafted western boot into the thick buffalo grass. "Because it wouldn't be right, going against Uncle Max's wishes. Especially not on the dream ranch he worked so hard to build. If he were here now, or if I'd had a chance to change his mind before he moved on to the next life, it would be different. But since that's not the case, I feel I have no choice but to go back to Denver to have my baby."

Josh's irritation with her rose. She was so damn lucky to have all the loving family she still did, and she didn't even know it. Resisting the urge to grab her and shake some sense into her, he dropped his hand from the tree trunk and stepped back, away from her. "Don't do that. Don't live your life by the wishes of those who are no longer with us," he said.

"Why not?" Noting a burr clinging to the knee of her trim, dark blue jeans, Patience bent down to pick it off, toss it aside.

"Because it's wrong. You've got to let go, Patience, of Max and Alec Vaughn. You've got to do what is right for you." That was what Max had wanted for her, for her to move on and stop living just half a life. Josh knew the only way he could get Patience to do this, as difficult and potentially treacherous as it was going to be for him, was to make her forget Alec Vaughn had ever even existed.

Patience's blue eyes took on a recalcitrant gleam as she noticed a burr on the sleeve of his shirt and picked it off, too. "I thought I'd made it clear I don't want your advice on this or anything else, Josh."

"I know you don't, but you're going to get it anyway. Which is probably why your uncle picked me as the potential father to your heirs," Josh finished. "Because I call them the way I see them."

Patience took advantage of the opening given. "Other than to express your initial surprise, which mirrored mine, you haven't said how you feel about that," she remarked curiously, all too aware she was pushing the envelope a little.

"About what?"

"Being the father of my children." Patience tilted her chin at him and tested the waters bravely. "Combining our genes."

The hint of a smile tugged at the corners of his lips as he looked her up and down. "It isn't something I'd planned on," he drawled finally.

"But?" Patience couldn't resist prodding.

Once again, his sexy glance drifted to her feminine curves before returning to her face. "I admit the idea of it—and I'm talking in a strictly speculative sense now—has a certain appeal."

One look at the rapacious glint in Josh's long-lashed, silver-gray eyes told Patience he was talking about sex. Not babies and diapers and getting up to rock and feed the little darlings in the middle of the night. The two were absolutely not one and the same to her. In fact, she had fervently wished on more than one occasion that she could forgo the actual making of the baby altogether and go straight to having the baby and holding him or her in her arms.

As she became aware that Josh was waiting for her reaction to his teasing, she felt her cheeks grow warm. She propped her hands on her hips and scolded him. "We're not talking about the process of making babies, Josh."

Aren't we? his look plainly said. He shifted a strand of hair away from her face, his expression glimmering with suppressed amusement. "It's hard to get pregnant without making love."

"Not necessarily," Patience corrected archly.

His sexy smile broadened as he leaned in close. "Trust me on this, Patience. There are some areas in which the old-fashioned way is best. And you may as well know now—" he trailed a hand down her face "—I'm an old-fashioned kind of guy, especially in that sense."

Patience had half suspected Josh would react this way, once he got over the shock of Max's plans for them. Unfortunately, to her immense chagrin, Patience found it all too easy to conjure up an image of her and Josh, locked in a passionate embrace, making love—making babies—as if there truly were no other way to achieve her lifelong dream of having a child of her own. Fortunately, she knew better. She had researched the ways to have a child without a mate. And there were plenty of those that did not involve her and Josh touching each other at all.

Apparently, Josh realized that, too, for he frowned abruptly and cast a look at the sky, which was turning a dusky blue-gray, with streaks of red and pink near the horizon. Reluctantly, he dropped his hand, moved away. "We better get back if we want to get in before dark."

Not surprisingly, they were silent as they rode back, both caught up in their own thoughts.

Josh was an expert horseman. Patience enjoyed riding with him at a sedate pace. She enjoyed it even more when she urged her horse into a gallop and Josh and his mount kept pace.

Side by side, they raced back toward the ranch, slowing only as they rode into the yard and headed for the stable where the riding horses were kept. Josh was there to help her down from the saddle.

"I can do this myself," Patience said a little breathlessly.

Josh gazed down at her. "I know," he said softly. But he made no effort to remove his hands from her waist.

Warmth from his touch filtering through her, Patience could only stare up at him. Who knew how long they would have stood like that if not for the sound of a distinctly feminine cough behind them.

They turned in unison. Patience felt Josh tense as a beautiful, dark-haired woman in her late thirties moved to join them. She was clad in jodhpurs, a silk blouse and a velvet-collared tweed blazer. Her short, burnished mahogany hair was styled in sophisticated two-inch layers. Patience had only to look at her to realize that she was a Silver Spur Ranch customer, probably from the city, and probably there to see or buy a horse on the premises.

"Josh, hi," the attractive woman said. "I've been waiting to talk to you."

Josh dropped his hands from Patience's waist, stepped back. "Nice to see you, Ms. Diehl. But this really isn't a good time—"

Ms. Diehl's smile remained fixed, but Patience could sense the tension flowing between them. "It won't take long," Ms. Diehl assured Josh. "I just wanted to let you know that I'm here for the weekend. I'll be bunking in the guest quarters, as usual."

"You come here often?" Patience interjected, more curious than ever.

"At least once a month. I'm Holly Diehl. I have a brood mare stabled here. Sapphire isn't due for another three months. But I try to visit her whenever I can, and keep an eyes on things."

And that included Josh, too, Patience was willing to bet. Was this what Cisco had meant when he warned her to be careful? she wondered uneasily, before her good manners took over and she did what Josh had purposefully, she was sure, neglected to do. "Hello, Holly," Patience said with a warm smile. "And welcome. I'm Patience McKendrick."

Holly nodded at her graciously, then paused, her hazel eyes sobering. "I read about your Uncle Max in the Butte newspapers," she said compassionately. "Please accept my condolences."

"Thank you," Patience said.

"Max is really going to be missed around here," Holly continued.

"By all of us," Josh inserted solemnly.

For a moment they were all silent, sad. Josh looked at Patience expectantly. "Are you ready to get the horses put away for the night and go in?"

Patience nodded, knowing Josh had just given her permission to move on, but she didn't want to miss any of what was going to be said, and so she just waited at his side.

Patience sensed Josh was not pleased with her behavior, but there was no evidence of that as he turned back to Holly. "Sapphire's doing fine," he told Holly bluntly as the two of them locked gazes. "There's no reason for you to worry."

Was it her imagination, Patience wondered, or were those words of Josh's heavy with meaning other than just the obvious?

"Still—" Holly pinned Josh with a casual look as she retorted just as smoothly " —I'd like to talk to you in person about the recent changes."

"No problem. I'll be glad to go over everything with you in detail tomorrow," Josh said bluntly. "In the meantime, Soaring Eagle would be glad to show you the farm records or answer any questions you might have about her care since you were last here."

"Thanks," Holly said easily. "I'll do that."

Holly thanked Josh politely, said goodbye to them both and walked away, leaving Patience to wonder if there was anything between Holly and Josh after all. She knew she wouldn't rest until she had identified the source of the tension she had felt between them earlier. "So, what's between the two of you?" Patience asked as she and Josh unsaddled their horses and went about the business of briskly rubbing them down. "That exchange seemed a little . . . personal."

To Patience's relief, the heated denials she half expected from Josh never came. "I think Holly is concerned about me in the same way I'm concerned about you, in the same way anyone is concerned about someone else who's recently suffered a loss. Then, too, maybe she wants reassurance that the quality of care here will not change just because Max is gone."

That made sense, Patience knew. She expected many more such calls in the days to come. Still, her radar was telling her there was more going on here than appeared on the surface. She made sure her horse had water and feed, then closed the stall door. "Does Holly usually stay the weekend when she visits Sapphire?"

Josh shrugged. "A lot of the owners who've bred their horses to our stallions and are waiting for their mares to give birth to their foals here stay over. Particularly when they have to drive long distances to get here. You know that."

Yes, Patience did. In fact, they had a row of guest quarters between the bunkhouse, where the hired hands who resided on the premises lived, and the manager's cabin, where she assumed Josh had been living since taking over the position. Nevertheless, she couldn't shake the gut feeling that there was more going on between Josh and Holly Diehl than Josh was willing to say.

"Ready to go on back to the house?" Josh asked as they left the barn.

Patience nodded. "If you don't mind, I think I'd like to turn in early tonight. Soon, actually."

Josh glanced at his watch. "It's only eight o'clock!"

Patience strode up the tree-lined path to the log cabin with its attached writing studio. The closer they got to what were more than likely going to be far too intimate quarters for the two of them, the harder her heart raced. "I know, but it's been a long, stressful day."

Josh continued to size her up as they approached the steps. He lifted a brow. "Sure you're not just running?"

Chapter Three

Dear Patience,
I never got over a long-lost love. What should I do?

Sincerely,
Lost in the Jungle of Love

Dear Lost in the Jungle of Love,
Get over it. Time marches on and so should you.
Looking for My Own Special Tarzan, Too,
Patience

"What could I be running from?"

"Lots of things."

"Such as?"

"The past. The present. Even me. Or maybe it's the news about Alec—and what you found out tonight," he speculated, pinning her with a soft, searching gaze.

"You're right." Patience sighed as she stopped to admire the gardenia bushes that rimmed the house. They were in full bloom, the fragrant white blossoms filling the air around them with a heady, perfumed scent. "I haven't had much time to deal with it." She paused, her hand on the porch railing that bordered the steps. She was suddenly reluctant to go inside, to make their sharing quarters, at least for the next two days and two nights, official. "That's why I was thinking maybe a long soak in a hot bath and an early bedtime would help me deal with things." She hadn't had supper yet and she wasn't actually sleepy, but he didn't know that.

"Then Max was right," Josh said softly, looking amazed that anyone could carry a torch for a lost love for seventeen years. "You really weren't over Alec, were you? And after all this time."

Patience flushed with embarrassment. She hadn't meant to reveal herself that way to Josh, or anyone else for that matter. Besides, as an advice columnist to the lovelorn who made her living telling others not to be saps in their personal relationships, she had a reputation to maintain. Her spine stiffened. "Whether I am over Alec or not—" and Patience admitted to herself there were days and nights when she did not think she ever would be "—it's really none of your business, Josh."

"Isn't it?" Josh reached past her to pluck a gardenia blossom from the bush. "I'm supposed to marry you in less than forty-four hours." He stripped the stem of leaves and placed the white blossom behind her ear. "At the very least we're going to be business partners, Patience."

He was taking too much for granted. Stepping in where he had no right. She had to find a way to put a halt to that, pronto. She slipped into ice-maiden mode, knowing it was her best, most effective defense. "Unless I choose not to inherit." And that was a possibility, Patience thought stubbornly, plucking the gardenia blossom from her hair, if this did not work out.

He watched as she lifted the blossom to her face. "I thought you intended to honor Max's wishes."

Patience dropped the blossom to waist level and shrugged. "That was before I got to know you," she answered haughtily, very much aware they were getting way too close, way too fast. She didn't know quite how he had done it, but Josh had gotten an awful lot out of her in a very short time, while at the same time revealing next to nothing about himself or his own relationships. That, too, was dangerous. She hadn't known Alec very long when she had gotten involved with him, either. Yet he had done the same thing. Managed to get very close to her very quickly.

"You still don't know me," Josh pointed out casually, picking another blossom, and then another, and another, handing them over one by one until she was holding a bouquet.

Aware that she felt suspiciously like a bride, and that maybe he wanted her to feel that way, Patience merely held her ground and shrugged. "And maybe that's the way it should stay?" she suggested lightly, refusing to take him—or this marriage business—seriously. It was a baby she wanted these days, not a husband.

She looked at him pointedly. "Besides, you're invading my space."

He grinned. "And if I'm around, I'll keep on invading it," he promised. "So deal with it, Patience. *Deal with me*."

She grinned back and coquettishly shook her head at him. She didn't know quite how he had done it, but Josh had not only taken away her sadness, he had them flirting. Nevertheless, she didn't want him getting too cocky. "Somehow, I don't think this was in Max's plan," she told him drolly.

"Wrong again." Josh plucked another flower and added it to her bouquet. "I think this was exactly Max's plan," he whispered with a knowing glance. "I think he wanted you to have more man than you could handle, right off the bat."

Josh was certainly that, Patience thought as her insides warmed and her heart began to race. It wasn't going to be easy sharing space with him, never mind platonically, even for the next day and a half. She could already tell. Which made her all the more reluctant to go inside.

She looked him over from head to toe and couldn't help but note what superb physical shape he was in beneath the rough ranch-hand clothes. "Shyness is obviously not one of your problems."

Josh laughed softly. "Guess not."

Their gazes meshing, they regarded each other in breathless silence. Patience was aware that it was getting dark. And that she alone had the key to get into the house. If they waited much longer...

"Hey, Doc!"

Patience breathed a sigh of relief. A distraction!

She and Josh turned in unison to see Rusty striding toward them. Oblivious of the sexual tension that had been flowing like a fast-running river between her and Josh, the veteran ranch hand was anxious to relate his news. "Sorry to bother you, Doc... Patience." Rusty tipped his hat at her, then turned back to Josh. "But Foxy Miss, that new bay mare that shipped in late today, seems to have a little swelling in the right foreleg tonight. Thought you might want to have a look at her afore you bed down for the night."

"You're right. I do." Josh turned to Patience expectantly.

She thought she knew what he was going to say and couldn't exactly say she was sorry about the reprieve, even if it was only temporary. "I know," she said, reading his mind with a smile. "Whither thou goest, I go. At least for now," she amended, tongue in cheek.

"Thanks." Now that there was a problem to be attended to, he seemed anxious to get going. "It shouldn't take long."

"NEVER A DULL MOMENT around here, is there?" Patience asked as she accompanied Josh into the stables that housed Foxy Miss.

"One of the charms of the place, in my opinion," Josh retorted, trying not to notice how pretty Patience looked in her riding gear. Trim but not overly tight, her dark blue denim jeans outlined her long, sexy legs to advantage. The white silk tunic she wore was long and full, blousing almost to midthigh. She wore a short suede vest, one shade darker than the pale, wheat gold color of her hair, over that. Knee-high boots of the same soft-hued leather. The outfit shouldn't have been that sexy. And maybe it wouldn't have been on anyone else. But ever since the moment he had laid eyes on her, coming out of the house for their ride, Josh had had all he could do to keep his hands to himself.

He wanted to take her in his arms. He wanted to slip his hands beneath the vest and her blouse and trace all of her soft, supple curves. And most of all, he wanted to tease her and goad her until she forgot all about the past and concentrated only on the present. He wanted to kiss her senseless until she thought only of the present.

Aware she was watching his every move, waiting for him to elaborate, Josh slipped into the stall ahead of her and explained, "I like being busy."

Patience nodded as he stepped closer to Foxy Miss, who, after her long ride in the horse trailer, still seemed a little skittish.

Patience watched as Josh stroked Foxy Miss's mane and whispered to her softly, telling her all he was going to have to do to check her out.

When she had settled down, he hunkered down beside her to have a look at her foreleg. Rusty had been right. It was swollen. It needed to be bandaged.

"What do you need?" Patience asked.

"Some liniment and a crepe bandage," Josh said. "They're in the first-aid trunk, in the tack room."

Patience returned breathless seconds later, her cheeks pink from the energy expended. "Here you go."

Their hands brushed as Josh took both items, giving him another jolt. "If you'll stroke her mane, I'll do the rest," he said, checking his reaction to her nearness.

"Sure thing." Murmuring soft, soothing words, Patience stepped into the stall.

Free to focus simply on the injury—which was, from the looks of things, more than likely a temporary condition caused during the transport—Josh carefully applied liniment and wrapped the foreleg. Finished, he put the materials away, washed up and went back to join Patience, who was still speaking in dulcet lullaby tones to Foxy Miss.

Seeing that Josh was waiting for her, and that Foxy Miss looked a little sleepy, too, Patience stepped out of the stall and shut the door behind her. "You were great," Josh said.

"So were you." Patience smiled. In fact, she thought as she joined Josh in the wide aisle, she hadn't really appreciated his talents on that score until just now, but he was obviously a wonderful veterinarian who had quite a way with animals.

"That being the case, I'd say a little congratulations are in order," Josh teased gently, taking both her hands in his. Just that swiftly, he bent toward her, their lips met, and before Patience knew it they were experiencing their first kiss. With all they had been through that day, all Max wanted them to share, Patience had expected he would kiss her, if for no other reason than to see if they were in the least compatible. And, knowing that Josh was the kind of man who did everything well and with full concentration, she had expected his first kiss to pack a wallop unlike anything she had ever felt. She had even expected herself to respond to the sensual, tender, seducing caress of his lips on hers. And she did.

But she hadn't expected the kiss to feel like a step back in time. And—heaven help her—it did.

His lips were soft, seductive and so sure.

Just like Alec's.

His breath was warm and staccato.

Just like Alec's.

He sifted his hands through the silk of her hair.

Just like Alec.

But, Patience thought almost hysterically, he wasn't Alec! Breathlessly, she tore her lips from his. Hands pressed against his chest, she levered herself away from Josh. She was trembling from head to foot as the blood drained from her face.

"What is it?" he demanded.

Patience drew in a shaky breath, very much afraid he would haul her back into his arms and kiss her again if she showed the least vulnerability to his embrace.

"Nothing," she fibbed.

But Josh, damn him, wasn't buying it. His brows drew together in thundercloud fashion. "It's him, isn't it?" he accused, sounding both amazed and bitterly resentful all at once. "You're still thinking of him!"

Patience flushed. What could she say to that? *Not only am I thinking of Alec, but I felt for one lost, helpless second that some small, deeply wonderful, deeply ardent part of Alec was still alive in you?* If she said that to Josh, he would think she was nuts. And maybe, Patience scolded herself shakily, she was. After all, these were not normal thoughts she was having. Nor was hers a normal response. Alec had been out of her life for years now, as Josh had pointed out earlier. Seventeen years. She should not still be carrying a torch for him. She should not be thinking of him when another man was kissing her. And she was. Why, she didn't know. No one else that she had kissed since the breakup had stirred up thoughts of Alec. So why Josh? Why now? Was it the passion? The fact that just one kiss from him made her tingle from her head to her toes. Or was it something else? Like her loneliness combined, in some odd way, with Max's passing and the crazy terms of his will. Terms that meant to see her married, pronto—to Josh, no less. Or was it simply the news that Alec was dead, the knowledge that she would never see him again, that had her conjuring up his ghost?

Josh's eyes remained full of questions she had no desire to answer. "I have to get out of here," Patience said. *Before I lose my mind, if I haven't already.*

She swept past him and ran out into the night. Josh was fast on her heels. Catching up with her as they neared the rear doors of the studio, he caught her arm and tugged her around to face him. "Patience, listen to me. Max was right. You can't go on like this."

Patience balled her hands into fists and released a frustrated breath. "Tell me something I don't know."

He clasped her shoulders, crowding her and forcing her to face him when she would have bolted. "Let go of the past, Patience," he ordered in a low, gruff voice.

He didn't know what he was asking! Patience shook her head and replied in a low, anguished voice, "I can't." Didn't he think she had already tried, over and over again?

"I'll be the judge of that," he murmured, dropping his hands from her shoulders to her back and taking her into the strong, warm cradle of his arms again.

And this time, as he kissed her, there was nothing of Alec in the embrace—if there ever had been. There was only Josh. Only the fierce pressure of his lips on hers, the warm cage of his arms, the demanding hardness of his body. He kissed her and kissed her until she felt like swooning, until she clung to him and whimpered low in her throat, until she kissed him back the way he was kissing her, with every fiber of her being. And only then, only when she had surrendered herself to the moment, and to him, and whatever it was they were sharing, did he let her go.

She stumbled backward, her hand pressed to her lips. Again, she was shaking from head to toe, as much from what she had felt as what she hadn't.

How could it be, she thought, that he had kissed her twice in the space of ten minutes and the two experiences were totally different? How could she have felt this man—this strong, hell-for-leather cowboy—was in any way connected to the gentle and sensitive Alec she had once known and loved? The two were as different as night and day. Which meant . . . what? Was she losing it? Or was there something—some connection between the two men—mystical or otherwise—that she was feeling in her heart, in her gut, that she just wasn't able to identify? Patience wondered. Or was this all because of something much more basic, something Josh—with all his intuitiveness where she was concerned—was already seeing? Was it all because she was reluctant to go on, to risk her heart and soul again for fear she'd be left at the altar? Again.

"It's going to be an uphill road for us, isn't it?" Josh guessed grimly, towering over her.

Patience shrugged and figured for both their sakes that she might as well be one hundred percent honest about that, even if she had to do it wryly. She picked up the bouquet of gardenias she had left on the steps earlier. "Did you really think, given the terms of Max's will, it'd be anything but?"

"Guess not." He paused as she got her house key out of the pocket of her jeans. Without warning, his look turned almost unbearably compassionate. "Look, you were right earlier, when we first started to go inside. It has been a long, grueling day, for you especially. So feel free to take your time in that bath you wanted earlier," he said, lounging against the railing as she unlocked the door. "I'm not sure there's any of that lavender soap you like around. There's not much call for it among the men, but—"

Patience stopped in the act of opening the door, her inner warning system on full alert once again. She swung around to regard him incredulously. "What's wrong?'' Josh asked, clearly having no clue. Her low voice reverberating with suspicion, Patience advanced on him and demanded, ''How did you know I liked lavender soap?''

Chapter Four

Dear Patience,
My fiancé thinks I am less than perfect in a million tiny and not so tiny ways. What should I do?
                                    Sincerely,
                                    Hopelessly Flawed

Dear Hopelessly Flawed,
If you have to change everything about you to be
the woman in his life, he's not the man for you,
and you're not the woman for him. Chalk it up to
a bad match, honey, and head for a new and better trail.

                        Getting the Heck Out of Dodge, Too,
                                    Patience

"Max must've mentioned it," Josh said.

Patience regarded Josh, so stunned she could barely
speak. "Max didn't know." It was something she'd
picked up and then later abandoned her first year of
college.

"Then someone here on the ranch," Josh suggested.

Patience's pulse jumped erratically. "No one here
knows that, either," she said.

"But I did," Josh retorted, persisting amiably. "And I must've gotten that knowledge from somewhere."

"My point exactly," Patience muttered as she led the way into her writing studio. That eerie I've-just-landed-in-the-twilight-zone feeling of déjà vu was hitting her stronger than ever.

Josh shrugged. "Then maybe it was an unconscious thing."

He glanced around cursorily at the comfortable oak office furniture and state-of-the-art computer, laser printer, fax, phone and copier. A coatrack, small television and stereo took up one wall, bookshelves and oak file cabinets two others, floor-to-ceiling windows another. Unable to shake the feeling something suspicious was going on here, Patience sank into the padded swivel chair behind the desk.

"Maybe I noticed the scent of lavender on your skin or in your hair," Josh continued.

He certainly had been close enough, Patience thought as she struggled to take command of the situation. There was only one problem with that theory. She tapped the toes of her boots against the edge of her desk. "I don't use lavender soap anymore, Josh."

His composure intact, he continued to look at her. "How come?"

Because Alec gave me a whole case of it the one and only Christmas we were together. And I unceremoniously tossed it all out when he jilted me, along with nearly everything else he had given me. "Because I associate lavender soap with my freshman year in college and I've outgrown it."

Josh's gray eyes lit up with a distinctly male, distinctly sensual interest. "What fragrance do you wear, then?" he asked softly.

"Chanel No. 5."

He sat on the edge of her desk, leaned in close to her and drew a breath. "I wouldn't have recognized it—I'm no expert on perfumes, but it's . . . nice."

Hand on his chest, holding him at bay, Patience kept her eyes on his and refused to be distracted. "That still doesn't explain how you knew I was once crazy about lavender soap." And she was far too shrewd to be convinced it was a lucky guess on his part.

"I know," Josh retorted with mock solemnness. To Patience's frustration, he didn't seem to be trying all that hard to recall the basis of his startlingly intimate knowledge of her. "Guess it'll always be a mystery," he continued. "Not that I am all that surprised I have a tidbit like that randomly stored away in my memory bank." He picked up a glass paperweight from her desk and shifted it from hand to hand. "The men around here never stop talking about you, you know. It's always Patience this and Patience that. . . ."

Patience plucked the paperweight out of his hands and put it back on her desk. "That's because I spent a lot of time hanging out at the horse operation when I was a kid. The old-timers like Slim and Soaring Eagle are all surrogate family to me."

Josh paused and looked around behind him at the dictionary and thesaurus Max had supplied for her. "Is it possible one of those guys—say, Slim or Rusty, for instance—noticed the scent of lavender on your skin when you were home for a visit while you were in college, at Christmas or something, and remarked on it, only to have you tell them that it was the new soap you were using?"

"Maybe." Patience hesitated. "I don't really recall that ever happening—"

"But it could have," Josh said.

"Yes," Patience admitted with a shrug. "I mean, they're not shy about paying me compliments. They do that nearly every time they see me. These days they're always telling me I look great, or something. When I was growing up, they remarked on it every time I grew an inch or changed my hair."

Briefly, Josh's glance turned envious. "You're lucky to have so many who've loved and watched over you through the years," he murmured enigmatically.

"I know," Patience replied, pushing to her feet once again. She sighed as she looked around the writing studio. Clearly, Uncle Max had gone all out for her here. "If only—"

Josh rose and followed her to the windows. "What?"

Patience stared out at the velvety black darkness. "If only I could just meet the man of my dreams," she said softly. *And maybe, just maybe, I did today?...*

Josh shifted restlessly beside her. "Or more specifically, the man who will replace Alec?"

Patience didn't like the low edge of jealousy in his voice. She turned so the row of floor-to-ceiling windows was at her back. "You are overstepping your bounds here, Josh," she warned.

He took her in with a narrow-eyed glance and suggested in a low, insinuating tone, "Maybe it's time someone did."

Patience bristled. If Josh had meant to get her full attention, he just had. "What is that supposed to mean?" she demanded.

"This guy Alec ditched you at the altar, right?" Patience would have preferred to forget that, but it was easier said than done when she could still recall what was to have been her wedding day with devastating clarity, just like it was yesterday. It had been Valentine's Day, and it was snowing, and she was standing there in the most incredibly beautiful white satin wedding gown and veil.

"HE'S LATE. He's really late," Patience worried aloud to Cody and Trace as she paced the small anteroom adjacent to the vestibule.

"Maybe he got caught up in traffic," her older brother, Trace, suggested.

Patience shook her head, feeling desperate and near tears. She was sure something was wrong. "His dorm is three blocks from the church. He could have walked here and back ten times by now and he's always on time."

"Look, we'll go out and see if we can find him," her younger brother, Cody, offered after a moment as he picked up on the depth of her unease.

Again, Patience shook her head. "His roommate, William, has already done that. Besides, Alec'll show up," she reassured them all fervently as she clutched her bouquet with trembling fingers. *"I know he will."*

But to her increasing mortification and embarrassment, Alec didn't show up. Not that half hour, or the next, or the next. An hour and a half after the ceremony was to have begun, the minister came back to where she was still waiting. Patience could hear the organist playing valiantly in the background. Above that was the murmur of voices, which were growing louder and more distressed by the moment. "My dear..." the minister said gently, taking her hands.

Patience gulped. She had a feeling she knew what he was going to say. Worse, she felt like a fool in the elaborate wedding gown she had spent hours picking out, to

*the detriment of all her college classes. She faced the
minister with as much courage as she could muster,
knowing her cheeks were hot with embarrassment and
had been that way for hours now. "Still no word?" she
asked, hoping to hear something different.*

*"His roommate just got back. He wants to speak to
you."The minister smiled and left to get William.*

*"If he's jilted you," Cody murmured beneath his
breath, looking even more hot-tempered than usual, "I
swear I'll kill him!"*

*"Take a number and stand in line," Trace added
dangerously. Turning to her, he patted her shoulder like
the intensely protective older brother he was. "Cody's
right. If Alec Vaughn has jilted you, he's dead meat.
You won't have to worry about him bothering you ever
again. Cody and I'll see to that." Trace compressed his
lips grimly. "Hell, we'll even get Max to help!"*

*The sound of a throat clearing had them all looking
up. "Well?" Patience asked Alec's roommate anxiously. "What were you able to find out?" Please, she
thought, tell me he's fallen on the ice and broken his
ankle. Tell me his tux didn't fit and he had to run to the
formal wear shop to get another one, or that he over-
slept. Tell me anything except he's not coming!*

*William's shoulders sagged. "I didn't want to tell you
earlier, because I was hoping I was wrong and I didn't
want to upset you, but now it looks like I've got no
choice. Alec left campus the night before last. He took
a suitcase with him."*

*Patience's heart was pounding but she forced herself
to stay calm and not jump to any conclusions just yet.
Alec hadn't mentioned any trip to her, but there was
probably a perfectly logical explanation for that, as he
never did anything without a damn good reason. He*

was the type of person who always, always thought things through. That was one of the things she loved about him. "Where was he going?"

William shrugged reluctantly and tugged at the starched white collar of his tux. "He didn't say. He just asked me to cover for him in case you called yesterday or this morning. So I did, telling you he was at the library, working on that paper he had due today, or in the shower, but I swear to you, Patience, Alec never said anything about not showing up for the ceremony. 'Cause if he had, well, you know I would never be part of hurting you."

And William hadn't. Alec had.

"So you never saw Alec again after that." Josh's voice brought Patience gently back to the present. "At least so far as Max knew," he added.

Finding the small but well-appointed room claustrophobic, she pushed on out into the hall and into the adjacent living room of the two-story log cabin home. It was small but cozy, with deep cranberry red sofas, glowing wood floors and colorful rag rugs scattered throughout. Patience stepped around the suitcases and the cat carrier she had brought in with her upon arrival but had not bothered to take upstairs and put away. A quick glance around revealed that her Persian cat, Tweedles, who did not much care for strangers, had taken cover at the sound of voices—probably upstairs.

"How could I?" she asked Josh quietly in return, surprised to hear her voice sound so normal when her heart was aching so. "I couldn't find him."

For a moment, Josh went absolutely still. Then he moved to the fieldstone fireplace and lounged against it negligently, bracing his shoulders against the mantel. "You're saying you looked?"

Patience shrugged one shoulder, briefly averted her glance and turned away. "I had to deal with his college roommate," she explained, aware her voice had turned a little defensive. "William was supposed to notify me the moment Alec showed up again, so I could go over and confront him in person."

"Only Alec never showed," Josh guessed without inflection.

"Not even to collect his things." Patience passed a hand over her eyes. "He didn't finish the term," she continued numbly. "Didn't come back for anything." Not that year or any other while she was still at Yale. Nor had he transferred to another university, because Patience had checked. It had been as if he had fallen off the face of the earth the day he decided not to marry her. And for that, she couldn't help but think that maybe she had ruined a part of his life as much as he had ruined a part of hers.

"Max figured if that happened it was probably for the best. In fact, he hoped you would never see him."

Patience sighed. "So did I, after a while." In fact, for a while—when she had finally realized he wasn't coming back to her, not ever—she had really hated Alec.

"I disagree. I think you should have had your day to confront him."

Something in his low voice got to her. Patience tipped her face up to his. "What makes you so sure of that?" she asked. She was beginning to understand why Max had confided in Josh about something so personal. When it came right down to it, he was easy to talk with. Compassionate, too.

"It's just nature," Josh said gently, moving away from the fireplace and following her to the sofa. He covered her hand with his own. "We see it when the worst happens and a mare delivers a dead foal. The mare won't stop looking for her foal until she has a chance to nuzzle the stillborn baby and experience the death and sense of loss firsthand. It's the same for humans. And since you never had a chance to confront Alec for jilting you, maybe that, and not any lingering love, is what has kept you from really moving on with your life."

Patience knew the lack of closure, of any final illuminating argument with Alec, would haunt her forever.

"You want my advice?" Josh asked finally.

There was no point in feeling sorry for herself, Patience knew. Her chin took on a stubborn tilt as she regained her equilibrium and retorted flippantly, "Absolutely not, but I suppose you're going to give it anyway."

"Move on. Be more cautious next time." Sensing correctly that she was about to bolt, Josh grabbed her hand and held on tight as he warned in a soft, serious voice, "You'll never be happy unless you let the past go, Patience. And that includes your memories and any lingering attachment to Alec Vaughn."

"WHY SHOULD I TAKE your advice?" Patience asked, making no effort to hide her disdain as she moved to extricate her hand from his. She couldn't believe Josh, a man she had just met, had the audacity to advise her on something so personal. "After all, when it comes right down to it," she pointed out calmly, "I don't know anything about you, either."

Josh watched as she stood, then followed suit. "That can easily be remedied. Ask away."

"Okay." Patience paused to probe his eyes, then went into the kitchen. Seeing Tweedles's milk dish was empty, she went to the refrigerator and got out a carton of milk. "Where are you from?"

"Prior to coming to the Silver Spur, I had a veterinary practice in Helena, Montana."

Kneeling, she wiped out the dish with a damp paper towel and filled it again. Aware of Josh's eyes upon her, cataloging her every move, she asked, "For how long?"

"One year."

"And before that?" Patience closed the carton, stood lithely and put the milk away.

"I worked at an animal hospital emergency room in North Dakota for six months, spent nine months on a ranch in Green River, Wyoming, and worked at a zoo in St. Louis for fifteen months."

"Have you worked anywhere else?"

"I was on another ranch in Utah for five months, another animal hospital—in Des Moines, Iowa—for twelve months. Before that, another veterinary practice, in Bloomington, Indiana, for seven months."

Patience thought she'd had a hard time settling down since her breakup with Alec. She had lived in several big cities while she was getting her career off the ground, but she had nothing on Josh. "So that's what Uncle Max meant in his will when he said it was time for you to stop drifting from place to place."

"He made no secret of the fact he thought I should settle down here." Josh opened the refrigerator and took out a single-serving bottle of orange juice. He uncapped the bottle and drank deeply, draining half of it in one gulp. Silence continued to reign between them.

"Feel better now that you know more about me?" he asked finally, glancing around at the small but serviceable old-fashioned kitchen.

Patience ran a hand along the glazed surface of the deep blue ceramic tile countertop. "Not necessarily. People who move around that much are either too footloose and fancy-free to ever make a permanent home in one place, or they're hiding something." She shoved her hands deep into the pockets of her jeans and, determined to keep their conversation on a light tone, asked in a deadpan voice, "Which is it with you?"

Josh braced his hips against the counter behind him and kept his eyes on hers. Clearly, he was not about to let her win this battle of wits. He volleyed a question right back. "Which do you think?"

Patience smiled, aware she hadn't felt this vibrantly alive or intrigued with a man in ages. "I think you're hiding something," she dared softly after a moment, wondering if he would take the bait and reveal even more about himself.

His expression didn't change, but for a moment he tensed at her goading remark and his eyes turned almost pewter. "What could I be hiding?" he asked calmly.

Until then, Patience wouldn't have guessed he was hiding anything. But something about the way he reacted to her flip remark...something about the look in his eyes...had her thinking maybe she was more on target than she knew.

Acting a great deal more nonchalant than she felt, she opened a can of tuna for Tweedles and decided to set that out, too. All too aware of the way Josh was tracing her slender curves with his gaze, she moved about her task. When she had finished, she straightened and rinsed out the tin before dropping it into the recycling bin. "Just out of curiosity, how did you end up working for Uncle Max?"

"I came by looking for work a couple of months ago. We met and he hired me full-time on the spot."

"It's not like Uncle Max to hire people off the street." Except for his attorney, Cisco Kidd, she amended to herself. Cisco was a different case entirely, Patience thought, because he had been rescued off the mean streets of Butte, Montana, when he was just sixteen.

Josh shrugged his broad shoulders carelessly as he drained the last of his juice and offered an explanation. "Max's staff veterinarian was getting ready to retire. He needed someone. I fit the bill. It was just that simple."

Nothing was that simple with Max, Patience knew. He had been as particular about who he hired as he had been about the horses he bought. No one had been more discriminating than Max. "Yet he knew your history. He knew you might quit?" Patience asked suspiciously. Max had not liked what he called short-timers. He had figured someone who planned to move on would not likely be as careful about the quality of his work as someone who planned to stay.

"He figured I might want to stay on permanently. If not, I promised to stick around and not leave him high and dry until he at least had time to find someone else."

"So you left your veterinary practice in Helena just like that." Patience found that, too, hard to believe.

"I found someone to take over for me."

"I find this all very strange."

"What can I say? I have a restless heart. And speaking of that restless heart, sometimes I just have to follow it." Before Patience could step back out of range, he had taken her in his arms once again.

She meant to fight him, she really did, but the moment his lips touched hers she was lost in the delicious sensations. With a low groan of desire, he parted her lips and swept the inside of her mouth with his tongue, again and again, until her heart pounded and her knees went weak and a deep ache started low inside her. Unwilling to go further, unable to hold back, she clutched at the soft white fabric of his western shirt. This was wrong. All wrong. And yet it felt so right, so incredibly let's-make-a-baby-this-instant right that she knew it had to end. "Josh—" She splayed her hands across the warm, solid wall of his chest. She couldn't let herself get tricked into believing that any of this was real, that he wanted her for any reason other than to gain his fifty percent share of the horse ranch. Because his work history proved he was not a man who stayed anywhere for long.

"Hmm?" Josh's lips left hers and forged a burning path across her cheek, down the nape of her neck, until it was all she could do to continue to resist.

"This is not a good idea," Patience said in a strangled voice as he continued to cloak her in his arms. Not when she was feeling so vulnerable. She pushed harder.

He released her reluctantly. "I suppose you're right." He sighed. "I suppose we should get cleaned up first, get something to eat." Patience didn't like the unspoken assumption that they would continue kissing, or whatever, later. "How about get cleaned up and get something to eat, period," she suggested firmly.

Josh snapped his fingers and humorously feigned distress. "Darn." His eyes met hers and held. "No baby making tonight, hmm?"

"None," Patience confirmed bluntly. She might be attracted to him. She might be his business partner one day and even be facing a short-lived but necessary marriage to him, all courtesy of Uncle Max. But she was *not* going to let him seduce her into making a baby with him until she'd had a chance to investigate his intentions toward her, the way she had never, and should have, investigated Alec's. She had taken his advice—to be cautious when falling in love with someone—to heart.

Chapter Five

Dear Patience,
My family thinks kids are the key to happiness
and they are pushing me to marry a man they approve of and have a baby, pronto. What should I
do?

Sincerely,
Not Quite Ready Yet

Dear Not Quite Ready Yet,
Family is all-important, but only you know when
it's time to marry and/or have your buckaroo. Tell
your family to step out of the ring. This is your
rodeo, no one else's.

Looking Out for Your Best Interests,
Patience

43:12

"You didn't tell me you had a dog," Patience said a few
minutes later when she came downstairs after her bath
and found Josh accepting delivery of a lively, seventy-
five-pound golden retriever with silky, buff blond hair
and enormous, soft black eyes.

Josh shrugged as he took over the leash. "You didn't ask. Thanks for bringing my gear over from the ranch manager's cabin, Slim."

"No problem, Josh. Let us know if you need anything else." Tugging the brim of his hat lower over his brow, Slim turned and disappeared down the front steps.

Josh shut the front door. "Now what?" she asked, wondering if he had any more surprises up his sleeve.

"I guess we make introductions. Goldie, this is Patience," Josh said, reversing the order of the introductions wryly. "Patience, Goldie."

"Very funny." Patience watched as Josh took the leash off his dog, who was busy sniffing out a red plaid dog cushion that had been set down on the hall floor next to Josh's duffel bag. She had known her forty-eight hours with Josh would not be easy, but this turn of events could mean disaster. "What about Tweedles, my cat?"

"I haven't seen her yet but I'm sure they'll get along. If not, we'll put them in separate rooms." He paused, looking reluctant to leave her.

His glance ghosted over the emerald silk lounging pajamas and satin ballet slippers she'd slipped on, and the way she'd swept up her hair into a loose knot on the back of her head. Patience knew she looked pretty and sophisticated in a way that was a bit too much for a casual evening at home on the ranch. But then that was the point. To show this cowboy they were worlds apart, and always would be. Maybe that, more than anything, would help keep him at arm's length. Lord knew she had to do something to keep him from kissing her again.

Patience swiveled away from Josh and shot a glance at Goldie, who had her red plaid cedar cushion clamped firmly between her jaws and was busy tugging it back toward the kitchen.

"Where'd you come up with a name like Tweedles, anyway?" Josh asked.

Patience felt Josh come up behind her, sensed the heat he radiated, even as she felt the warmth of his breath stirring her hair. It was a singularly luxuriant sensation, one she didn't dare give in to.

Swallowing hard, she tugged at the single strand of pearls around her neck and swung around to face him, a pleasant expression plastered on her face. "I didn't," she replied with more than necessary politeness. "Trace's two boys did." As she remembered how it had all come about, a trace of fondness crept into her voice and she related softly, "She was originally their kitten and they couldn't decide whether she was Tweedledee or Tweedledum, so they finally decided on Tweedles. Unfortunately, it turned out Trace was allergic to cats. So Tweedles needed a new home."

Josh shook his head sympathetically. "The poor kids must've been heartbroken."

"Right." Patience paused. She could have sworn, just by the way he looked at his pet and the rugged way in which he carried himself, that Josh was a dog lover through and through. It had been Alec who'd liked cats, because he'd had a kitten—the only house pet his father would allow—when he was a kid. She wet her suddenly dry lips. "You like cats?"

Josh shrugged, showing no emotion one way or another. "I love all animals. I'm a veterinarian, remember? Anyway, back to your story—" he prodded impatiently.

Aware she was digressing, Patience forced herself to get back on track. "Right. So I volunteered to adopt Tweedles, promised the kids they could visit her as much as they wanted, which they have, and Tweedles has been with me ever since." Patience smiled again, thinking about how much having a pet had brightened up her life and taken an edge off the loneliness she sometimes felt.

"Which has been how long?"

"About four years. Speaking of which, I better find her."

"Meantime, if it's okay with you, I'm going up to have my turn at the shower," Josh said.

"No problem." As far as Patience was concerned, the more time they spent apart, but still under one roof, the better.

"And don't let Goldie out alone, no matter how much she begs. She's in heat."

It was all she could do not to groan out loud. No doubt about it. The next forty-some hours were going to be extremely interesting. "That makes us just about even, then," she said sweetly, knowing she wasn't the only one who could bring on the surprises.

Josh paused in the act of unbuttoning his shirt and, edging closer, asked, "How come?"

Patience smiled. "'Cause my cat's pregnant and due any day."

"LOOKING FOR SOMETHING?" Cisco Kidd asked Patience as he headed up the front steps of the studio.

"Tweedles, my cat. She's about to have kittens and I haven't seen her since just before I left for Fort Benton this afternoon. She wanted out and I thought it would be okay. She's never been one to go very far, and there's a small pet door by the kitchen that she can use to get in and out all by herself. But now I'm wondering if it was such a good idea, letting her go out at all," Patience finished worriedly.

"She wouldn't go near the horses, would she?"

"No." Patience frowned. "Not unless she was chasing down a mouse or something."

"Want me to go and look for her?"

Again, Patience shook her head. "It probably wouldn't do any good. She's kind of shy around strangers. If she saw you coming she would just hide." Patience leaned against the porch railing, being careful to follow her Uncle Max's instructions and remain "under the same roof" as Josh. "If you see her, let me know."

"Will do," Cisco promised like the true friend he was.

"What brings you by?" Patience asked curiously. Though they talked often and had for years, she hadn't expected to see him this evening.

"I'm sorry. I know it's late, but I wanted to know how things were going."

Knowing he was only looking out for her, Patience quickly filled him in. Cisco listened tranquilly. His expression turned to a frown as she concluded, "Anyway, I got to thinking maybe Josh was right. Maybe I should check out the men I get involved with more thoroughly before I get involved. And I might as well start with him."

"I'll check into Josh's background for you."

Patience homed in on his skepticism. "But you don't expect to find anything, do you?"

Cisco tipped his Stetson back. "Max trusted Josh implicitly."

"Don't you find that strange? I mean, Josh had only been around a couple of months." And yet Max had put him in his will!

"That tells you something, too. Max was never a man who was all that quick to trust newcomers, unless he had a strong feeling in his gut. He felt that way about me. He felt that way about Josh. I have to think his feelings were continually substantiated or I know he wouldn't have done it."

Patience set her chin stubbornly. "I still want you to look into his background for me, see if the work history he told me checks out. And I want to know why he left all those jobs. Was it the result of his restlessness, or was he forced out?"

Cisco studied her closely. "You're really worried about this."

"I learned not to trust my gut instincts after I got involved with Alec," Patience whispered. "Because if I had done that, I never would have found myself in that awful situation . . . forced to take action."

She had walked to the front of the church on shaking legs, her beautiful wedding gown swirling around her. She was thankful her brothers were there with her, flanking her on either side as she undertook the ordeal of having to make the announcement herself. She had never in her entire life felt more deeply hurt and humiliated than she did at that very second.

Her face hot with embarrassment, she forced herself to face the friends gathered in the pews and nervously cleared her throat. Worse than their shock was their pity, which was coming at her in great unspoken waves. "If I may have your attention, please," she began, amazed her voice could be so cool and clear when her entire world was falling apart. "*I have something to say.*"

They waited while she wished desperately she could be anywhere else.

Temporarily losing her nerve, she looked at the vestibule doors of the church one last time, hoping against all reason to see Alec come bursting in. He didn't.

Aware she was on the verge of either bolting or becoming completely hysterical, she took a deep breath. It would all be over in a minute. Her impending marriage. Her prospects for a happy life. She smiled, aware she was beginning to feel a little faint. "Odd, now that I'm up here, I really don't know where to begin."

Trace took her hand in his. He leaned over and whispered in her ear, "Patience, honey, you don't have to do this."

Tears stinging her eyes, she shook her head in the affirmative. Yes, she did have to do this. It was the only way to hang on to what little was left of her dignity. To choose any other way out would be cowardly. And if there was one thing she had never been, she told herself sternly, it was a coward.

Lifting her chin a little higher, she did her best to ignore all the pitying looks directed her way. Might as well get this over with. It damn well wasn't going to get any easier. "I asked you all here to see me married today," she began, looking her audience in the eye. "With the exception of my Uncle Max McKendrick, you were all delighted to show up and offer your heartiest congratulations and best wishes." Patience snapped a rose out of her bouquet and crumpled it between her fingers. "I have to admit, I was furious with my Uncle Max for not believing I knew what I was doing when I said yes to Alec Vaughn's proposal. But it seems he was right after *all,''* she told her audience through tightly gritted teeth. *"Because I know now—"* the tears were beginning to start again *"—that Alec Vaughn is definitely not the man for me. If he were, he would have shown up here today. Maybe not exactly on time. Maybe not even to go through with the ceremony and marry me. But he would have at least shown up.''*

"Patience," Cody said, slipping an arm about her waist so she had no choice but to lean against his considerable shoulders. *"I think everyone gets the gist of things here. You don't have to say any more,"* he told her sternly.

But she did, Patience thought furiously. She owed the faculty and friends she had invited more than this, especially since they had been sitting here for so long, gamely waiting, trying for her sake not to act as if anything were terribly wrong, when they all knew it was.

"I'm sorry," Patience said, meaning it from the bottom of her heart. Two hours was really way too long to wait for a wedding to occur. *"Really, I am. Naturally, Alec and I—or actually, the way things are going at the moment, probably just me—will be returning all the gifts."* Keeping a stiff upper lip was getting harder. *"Thank you all so very much for coming."* She forced another smile. *"And now if you'll excuse me, I think I am going to take my brothers up on their offer and let them get me out of here."* Before I make even more a fool of myself. And, tears streaming down her face, she turned and fled.

CISCO WRAPPED a brotherly arm about her waist. "I'll see what I can do," he promised. "In the meantime, I'm here for you, as always."

"Thanks." Patience leaned into his hug. "I knew I could count on you."

Patience looked up to see Josh behind her. His face was impassive, but she had the feeling he was not happy to find his bride-to-be in Cisco's arms.

Maybe that was just as well, she thought philosophically, choosing not to correct his unspoken misimpression. She had been getting way too close to Josh, way too fast. It had only been a little over five hours since she had met him. Already, they had talked intimately and kissed numerous times.

Maybe the notion that she might already be emotionally involved with Cisco, on some level unbeknownst to her late Uncle Max of course, would be enough to keep Josh at arm's length. Or at least encourage him to proceed with his romancing of her more cautiously.

"Well, guess I better be going," Cisco said, responding to the new tension in the air.

Ignoring Josh's scowl of dismay, Patience smiled at Cisco. "Thanks for stopping by."

She and Josh stood together while he drove off. Josh turned to Patience. Clad in a pair of jeans and a fresh blue chambray shirt, he inclined his head toward the stairs. "There's something for you upstairs, in the back bedroom on the second floor."

Patience paused. She had no idea what he was talking about. "It was empty just a few hours ago, when I changed clothes before riding out with you to see the wild mustangs." She hadn't looked in there since.

"Well, it's not empty now."

"You going to tell me what's up there?"

He shook his head pragmatically. "I know it's late, nearly ten o'clock, and you're tired, but I still think you should see it yourself."

"I DON'T BELIEVE THIS," Patience breathed, hardly able to trust her eyes.

"Incredible, isn't it," Josh murmured as he lingered in the doorway beside her. "That they could do so much in so little time."

The once completely empty guest room had been turned into a nursery, with crib, changing table, dresser and a sturdy, burnished oak toy box that also doubled as a padded window seat. A brightly colored alphabet rug in a nubby cotton fabric covered the wood floor. A comfortable rocking chair sat in one corner. Scattered about the room were stuffed animals and toys. A note with her name on it was pinned to the pink-and-blue gingham baby quilt slung over one end of the crib.

Patience walked over to retrieve it. She smiled as she tore open the envelope and saw Max's familiar scrawl. Aware Josh was waiting anxiously, and that this probably concerned him as much as her, she read Max's message to her out loud.

"Dear Patience,
This is my way of letting you know it is okay with me if you come back to the Silver Spur to raise your baby, married or not. I think you're right. Any and all McKendricks should be brought up here. So do so and do it with my blessing.

　　　　　　　　　　　　Your loving uncle,
　　　　　　　　　　　　Max

P.S. Should you change your mind and decide to

provide said child with a daddy, Josh would make an excellent candidate.''

Patience took another sweeping glance around the room then looked at Josh mildly. ''How does he know?'' she murmured, folding the note and slipping it back into the envelope with fingers that trembled only slightly.

''What?'' Josh edged nearer.

She spread her arms dramatically wide. ''That you'd make an excellent candidate for a daddy?''

Josh shrugged, sure this was one argument he could win hands down. ''Seems to me I've got everything I need. Strong arms to carry both a baby and the overflowing bags of paraphernalia that go everywhere babies go. A shoulder that will serve as a pillow. A lap to sit on. I can change a diaper and warm a bottle with an efficiency that'd put even a British nanny to shame. I know first aid as well as a lullaby or two.''

''I see.'' Patience nodded with mock solemnness as Josh sank into the rocking chair and tried it out. ''And how are you at getting up in the middle of the night?''

''Superb.'' Josh picked up a stuffed panda and tried laying it against his shoulder as he would a baby. ''I can also read stories, play games, push a swing, a stroller, assemble a number of toys and bikes.''

''Getting a little ahead of ourselves, aren't we, Dad?'' Patience quipped dryly, plucking the stuffed panda out of his hands.

Josh shook his head confidently as he watched her put the panda on her shoulder. He bounded out of the chair and closed the distance between them. ''I don't think so. I think when it comes to rearing kids, the wise parent can never be too prepared," he counseled as he watched her put the panda back in the crib.

"You have an answer for everything, don't you?" Patience queried with grudging admiration.

His gray eyes gentled. "I try. And so apparently did Max. I don't think there's anything he forgot. He's even seen to the clothes and diapers and those tiny little undershirts—"

"It's called a layette."

"Whatever." Josh paused, aware there was a glimmer of moisture in Patience's eyes. "What's the matter?" he asked gently. "Don't you like it? Was it too presumptuous of Max?"

"No. It's perfect," Patience said thickly. She blinked rapidly as her voice dropped to a tremulous whisper. "And so like Uncle Max."

That was true, Josh thought. He had never met anyone more determined than Max to have his own way, except maybe Patience.

"Max doesn't pull any punches, does he?" Josh murmured thoughtfully. If all this didn't get Patience's baby lust going full blast, Josh didn't know what would, 'cause it was already doing dynamite things to his latent wish for a baby of his own.

"Max has never been afraid to speak his mind," Patience murmured, her lower lip trembling as she looked around her. Tears of joy filled her eyes.

"You okay?" Josh asked.

Patience nodded, unable to speak for a long moment. Her throat was clogged with tears. "It means a lot to me—that Max changed his mind on this and is giving me his blessing," she said finally.

JOSH STUDIED PATIENCE, wishing there was some way he could ease the ache in her heart. He knew that, happy as she was about Max's approval of her plans to have a family, she still missed him desperately. "You were close to him, weren't you?" he asked gently as he handed her a tissue, thinking maybe it would help her to talk about her relationship with Max.

Patience nodded and wiped her eyes. She sat down on the window seat, her expression reflective as she pulled herself together. "Max was very different from our dad, who was a reserved, kind of quiet guy and not at all flamboyant or eccentric," she confided softly. "But Max was just as loving and just as concerned about us and he tried his best to finish bringing us up the way he knew his brother would've wanted us brought up—with a great deal of emphasis on doing the right thing, and education and all that. In fact, in retrospect, I think that's one of the reasons why Max fought so hard for so long to keep me from having a child on my own. I don't think he felt my parents would've approved of that."

"Do you think that, too?" Josh asked, straightening the appliquéd quilt that was hanging on the side rail of the crib.

Patience lifted her slender shoulders in an eloquent shrug. "My parents were very conservative people. They firmly believed in marriage and family above all else."

"So they would've preferred you be married, too," Josh ascertained cautiously, wishing she didn't look quite so vulnerable, because that in turn made him feel all the worse.

"Yes." Patience lifted serious blue eyes to his. "But they also would have understood my yearning to have a child. They would have accepted the fact that I'm thirty-six and my time to do this is running out." She picked up a stuffed bunny and held it in her hands.

"But they wouldn't have expected you to marry someone you didn't love, just to provide your child with a father?" Josh queried, knowing that if he was ever going to understand Patience in the in-depth way he wanted to understand her, he had to know much more about her early life.

"No." Patience sighed, letting him know in an instant that she had changed as much as he had in the intervening years since they had last seen each other. "They knew that building a strong marriage is hard work, and that it requires a strong love at the heart of the relationship to be successful."

"So Max did as they would've wished, after all, in trying to keep you from making a mistake at first, and then supporting you in the end."

Reluctantly, Patience turned and replaced the bunny on the window seat beside her. "I guess so."

They were quiet a moment.

Finally, Patience looked up at Josh again. "You seem surprised."

Josh shrugged and figured he owed it to her to be honest about this much. He hunkered down in front of her, dropping to one knee. "To tell you the truth, I didn't know if I would like Max when I first headed out to the Silver Spur to look for work. I had heard many a tall tale about him. Legend was, there wasn't a smarter, more ambitious rancher and land baron in all of Montana."

"So you thought he might be a bad guy," Patience guessed.

"No. Bad guys are a different breed than Max," Josh mused, getting restlessly to his feet as, unbidden, the memories came back again, hitting him even harder. He had tried to forget the night that had forever changed his life. But being here with Patience, talking about the past, made that impossible. The memories of that night were as clear in his mind as yesterday, Josh thought, remembering how it had been. . . .

HE LAY FACEDOWN in the back of the van, every muscle aching from the ruthless pounding his body had taken. Tears of frustration and fury streaming down his face, he strained against the ropes biting into his wrists and ankles. To no avail. His fate, and that of the unconscious victim beside him, were sealed. . . .

He had seen and heard too much. They both had. There was no way the thugs were going to let either of them live, Josh knew. No chance in hell either of them would make it back for the wedding, no matter what he said or did. . . .

"THEN WHAT DID YOU THINK Max was going to be like?" Patience asked, her soft voice dragging him back to the present.

"I thought Max might be ruthless in the extreme. But when I got here and met him, and we had a chance to talk, I realized that he and I had a lot more in common than I would ever have expected," Josh continued.

For once, luck had been on his side. And it still was, he thought as he and Patience linked hands and left the nursery together.

"STILL NO SIGN OF TWEEDLES?" Josh asked Patience a few minutes later when she came in from the porch and they sat down to a late supper of cold fruit and sandwiches that he had assembled for them.

"No." Patience frowned as she spread spicy mustard on her roast beef. "And considering the late hour, I imagine she's curled up somewhere, asleep for the night.''

"Or has gone off to have her kittens in private," Josh said matter-of-factly, pouring them both tall glasses of milk.

Patience watched as Josh layered lettuce and tomato on his bread. "That's a pretty common occurrence, isn't it?"

At least he could offer comfort about this. "Cats are solitary creatures by nature. If that is the case, I'm sure she'll turn up soon enough," he said. "With all the hired hands we have working this ranch, someone is sure to spot her," he finished cheerfully.

"You're probably right." Patience breathed a sigh of relief. She glanced at Goldie, who was busy dragging her dog cushion into the kitchen, and couldn't help but smile at the antics of Josh's pet. "Now what is Goldie doing?" she asked.

"Looking for someplace cozy to bunk down for the night, I imagine," Josh said, aware it was a little comical.

"Does she always drag her cushion around like that?" Patience asked.

Josh nodded, feeling a flash of guilt for the way he'd moved his pet around with him, and he readily admitted, "It takes her a while to feel comfortable in any new place. When she finally decides where to keep her cushion and stops dragging it all over, I know she finally feels like she's home. And speaking of new homes . . . since it is almost midnight, I think we should talk about the sleeping arrangements." Josh leaned back in his chair. Difficult or not, this subject had to be broached. "As you may have noticed, there's only one comfortable bed here."

Twin spots of color appeared in Patience's cheeks as she lifted her eyes to his. "In the master bedroom. I know. Somehow I think Max planned it that way," she said dryly.

But to Josh's pleasure, she did not look all that displeased about the situation.

Josh shrugged and tried not to take too much for granted. Sharing the same bed was not the same as actually sleeping together and making love. "Thankfully, it's king-size. There's more than enough room for the both of us."

Patience had the feeling Josh expected her to play the part of the outraged maiden. She sat back in her chair and regarded him coolly. "You're suggesting we share?"

He drained his milk and decided to go for broke. "It makes more sense than one of us sleeping on the sofa," he retorted as he leaned farther back in his chair.

Not necessarily, Patience thought as she smiled at him. "Actually, I think you would be very comfortable there," she pointed out.

"Not as comfortable as in the bed. So what do you say?" Josh prodded, a challenging glint in his gray eyes. "Are you up to this or not?"

She knew he expected her to say no. Which in turn had some little imp inside her determined to prove him wrong and yearning to say yes. She shrugged carelessly, as if it did not matter to her one way or another. "Sure, as long as you stay on your side."

Finished with his meal, he got up to carry his plate to the sink. His mood was extraordinarily cheerful as they both silently contemplated the evening ahead. "No problem."

UNFORTUNATELY for Patience, sleep proved elusive. She lay in the darkened bedroom long after lights-out, tossing and turning. Despite her fatigue and the long, emotionally grueling day, she was unable to even approach sleep. Josh was much quieter, his breathing deep and even, his eyes closed, but she had the feeling he wasn't sleeping, either. Maybe because he hadn't bothered to undress and lay fully clothed on top of the covers on his side of the king-size bed, while she lay, still in her green silk lounging pajamas, which were decidedly not meant for sleeping in, beneath the covers on the far opposite side.

They could pretend this was normal, that they were sleeping in this bed as a simple matter of comfort and convenience. But they couldn't make it seem so. Not when she was close enough to breathe in the English Leather clinging to his skin and feel the warmth of his body stretched out next to hers. Worse, she knew from the way he kept tossing and turning that he was restless and wide-awake, too.

Without warning, there was loud barking on the front porch, soon echoed by some plaintive canine whimpering in the kitchen below. Curious, Patience got up and went to the window. Down on the lawn below she saw a large collie, still barking furiously.

Seconds later, Goldie appeared at the bedroom door. She came charging in, barking and pleading with Josh to go out. Josh swung himself lithely out of bed—confirming Patience's impression that he hadn't been asleep, either—and looked down at his dog sternly. "Quiet, Goldie."

Goldie ignored him and ran back out and down the stairs. There was a crash, followed by a high-pitched yelp.

"Now what?" Josh dashed down the stairs, Patience fast on his heels.

Patience switched on the light as they entered the kitchen. Goldie had her head and one shoulder stuck in the cat door. She was dancing around and whimpering in a lovesick way. The collie had come around and was yipping and barking excitedly on the other side.

Josh grasped Goldie by the shoulders and dislodged her from the cat door. "Lucky for us that opening isn't any wider or Goldie would be long gone," Patience drawled.

"I know," Josh said as the loud barking continued on the other side and Goldie still struggled to get out.

Josh peered out the back door window. "This is ridiculous. Wrangler, that's the neighbor's dog, I know because I gave him his rabies vaccination not too long ago—has to go back to his owner."

"Now?" Patience said. It was one in the morning!

Josh grabbed Goldie by the collar and held her firmly. "You have a better idea?"

"Has Goldie ever had puppies?" Patience asked as she and Josh tugged on their boots.

"No. She has a heart condition that would make giving birth dangerous for her."

"Poor Goldie," Patience said. How sad, she thought, to go through your entire life never knowing the joy of giving birth to a new life. If she wasn't careful, that could happen to her, too. Not because of any physical condition that prevented her from having a child while she could, but because she had been foolish enough to let her biological clock run out. And at thirty-six, Patience knew she did not have many childbearing years left.

"Unfortunately," Josh continued, "I've been unable to spay her for the same reason. The anesthetic necessary for such a procedure poses too much of a risk for her."

"So she knows what she's missing."

Josh nodded grimly. "And her biological clock is driving her crazy."

Much as mine is driving me crazy, Patience thought.

"But it'll be over soon," Josh continued as he put the retriever in the utility room, where she continued to bark and whine and beg to be let out. And they were out the door. "And then the window of opportunity for Goldie to get pregnant will be gone, too."

Just like mine will be gone, if I don't take advantage of the situation crazy Uncle Max set up for me and Josh, Patience thought.

Once outside, Josh whistled for Wrangler, but the collie refused to come. Instead he stayed just out of reach of Josh, darting back and forth and barking his head off.

"I think he knows you want to take him home," Patience murmured, not sure whether to be irritated or amused. There was a Romeo and Juliet quality to the two pets' attraction that she appreciated. Maybe because she had once been in a similar situation herself.

"Wrangler is right. I do want him back where he belongs before he rouses everyone in the bunkhouse and guest quarters, too." Josh turned to Patience and handed her the leash. "We're going to have to work together to round him up."

Anything to shut the lovesick pup up, Patience thought with a beleaguered sigh. "What do you want me to do?" she asked, more than willing to cooperate if they could only get some sleep!

"Go inside and bring back some sort of treat. A morsel of meat will do. I'll tempt him. When I collar him, you come up from behind with a leash and snap it on."

All too willing to work in tandem with Josh, Patience slipped back inside. When she returned, Wrangler had at least stopped barking. He was down on his haunches, face resting on his front paws, as Josh stood on the porch and spoke to him quietly. Patience handed over the beef. Having gained Wrangler's trust, Josh approached him and hunkered down in front of him about two feet away. Still talking softly, he held out the beef. Wrangler, who had apparently worked up an appetite while courting Goldie, wiggled forward on his tummy, and snatched the morsel from Josh.

Thus befriended, the collie allowed Josh to pet him, then take hold of his collar. Patience snapped on the leash and handed it to Josh. "Time to go home, Wrangler," Josh said firmly.

Wrangler looked up at him with liquid black eyes and let out another bark.

"Mission accomplished," Josh said some twenty minutes later as he and Patience drove away from the neighboring Lickety-Split Ranch.

Patience settled down in her seat and looked out at the passing landscape and velvet black sky, sprinkled with stars. A gentle summer breeze blew in through the open windows of the pickup. Maybe it was the beautiful star-filled night, maybe it was the company; she only knew she had never felt more content, not even in the days and nights she had been seeing Alec. And that was strange. Up until now, she hadn't thought anyone would ever be able to take Alec's place in her heart, yet Josh was quickly and effortlessly doing just that. Maybe

Max was right, Patience thought on a wistful sigh. Maybe it was time for her to move on and "dance with the one that brung you."

"This is my favorite time of night," Josh commented after a while.

Patience resisted the urge to scoot closer to him and lay her head on his shoulder while he drove. She knew she was getting far too romantically involved as it was. Yet, as she looked at him, he seemed smitten with her, too. And in an unexpectedly romantic mood. "You're out often after midnight?"

Josh grinned. "I'm out any time there's an animal emergency around here," he said.

"So I've been noticing." Patience turned toward him as much as her seat belt would allow. Her heart taking on a slow, heavy beat, she studied the rugged contours of his face and wondered once again how and why he had those tiny scars above his brows and the half-moon scar at the center of his lower lip. Had he been in a barroom brawl? she wondered with a journalist's curiosity. Or was there something else nefarious in his past? Something that to this day kept him moving on.

AN ODD AND UNEXPECTED feeling of contentment swept through Josh as he drove through the dark and silent Montana night toward home, Patience curled up in the passenger seat beside him.

Taking the lovesick Wrangler back to his owners had been a good idea. Sleeping in the same bed—perhaps "trying to sleep" would be a more accurate description of what had gone on between them earlier—had not.

Josh wasn't even sure why he had suggested it.

Sure, it was practical. No one wanted to get up all stiff and achy, and sleeping on one of the sofas would have guaranteed just that. But it had also been a test. Of his mettle and hers.

And it had been a long-held dream.

From the first time he had laid eyes on Patience, that one autumn years ago on the Yale campus, Josh had yearned to have her. No matter that she was out of his league, coming from such a wealthy Montana family. No matter that they had little in common. He had wanted her then. And he still wanted her now. To the point that for the first time in his life, Josh had an inkling of how it would feel to be in heat. Only in his case, Patience, not an overabundance of hormones and not the riches he stood to gain if he met the terms of Max's will, had inspired those feelings. Every inch of him was aching and yearning, not just for the physical release but for the soul-shattering feeling of completion that came with making love to someone you desired with every fiber of your being. And he did desire Patience.

The only question was, Would it ever happen?

Would Patience ever allow him to realize his long-ago dream of having her in his life?

More to the point, Josh thought as he turned the truck in the lane and headed toward the house, was the possibility even viable, considering all he could not— would not—ever tell her? About the past they had shared and the past they hadn't....

HE WINCED as he was hauled roughly out of the van and pushed into the passenger compartment of the waiting car. More disturbing than his own pain was the utter stillness of the body they were simultaneously shoving behind the wheel.

"This'll teach you to cross us," the thugs said, *laughing maliciously as they shifted the car into gear, slammed the doors and gave it a shove.*

He and his companion were over the cliff and airborne an instant later, plummeting slowly, inevitably down into the ravine—the car he'd had his first date in cartwheeling end over end. Swearing fiercely, he instinctively tried to shield his face, and praying hard for a miracle, he did his best to brace himself and his companion for the impact still to come.

"YOU REALLY ENJOY your work, don't you?"

Patience's low, sensual voice came at him as if through a fog. Glad to be home again, Josh parked the truck at the rear of the house, near her studio, and shut off the engine. He released the latch on his seat belt and turned toward her, in no hurry to go back inside. "Yeah, I do."

Patience released her seat belt, too. Lifting one foot to the seat, she linked both her hands around her ankle. Resting her chin on her raised knee, Patience regarded him curiously. "How and when did you decide to become an animal doctor?"

Josh rubbed a strand of her silky blond hair between his fingers. "It was shortly after I started college. I had to quit school for a while unexpectedly—money problems and so forth—and I ended up working at a humane society shelter in the interim. I wasn't a logical candidate for the job. I was a real city kid and had never even had a dog of my own. But I liked it. So much so that when I could afford to pick up my schooling again, I concentrated on veterinary medicine."

"It's funny how we fall into things sometimes," Patience said softly, leaning close enough for him to get a whiff of her perfume.

How well he knew that, Josh mused, his thoughts drifting back to the events he had just skimmed over. If not for a few hideously unforgettable days, he could have remained in school. Near Patience. But those days had happened and all he had to do was close his eyes to recall the stark horror he'd experienced. . . .

"I mean," Patience continued, bringing him back from the horror of the past and into the bittersweetness of the present, "I always knew I wanted to write. I just never imagined it would be advice."

He smiled at her, unable to help but think how beautiful she looked in the soft green silk, her eyes wide and soft, her hair shimmering pale gold in the moonlight. Looking at her was enough to make him forget. "You have a knack for it," he said gently, knowing it was true. Patience had a way of cutting right to the heart of the problem and offering solutions that pushed people forward, into the future, instead of keeping them locked into the unhappy present.

And the future was where he most definitely wanted to go. With her.

Patience climbed out of the cab of the Silver Spur Ranch pickup truck, as did he. She circled around the back of the truck, meeting him at the tailgate. "You've been reading my column," she teased.

Josh smiled down at her, knowing he wanted nothing more than to make love to her, again and again and again. "I think the question is, Who hasn't read your column? You're syndicated in papers all over the country."

"One hundred and fifty-two, at last count."

"Max was very proud of you for that." As was Josh, who knew from everything her uncle had told him that Patience had earned every success through years of hard work and the expense of her personal life.

Patience ducked her head shyly. "Uncle Max admired ambition."

That he had. Wanting to see her smile again, Josh took her hand and playfully tugged her close. "You know what he told me? He said you had moxie."

Patience tilted her chin at him, mischief slipping into her answering grin. "He did, did he?"

Josh let his glance rove her face, memorizing every beautiful inch of it. "He also said he worried about you when you were a kid. He had a hard time reading you."

Unbidden, sadness crept into her vivid blue eyes and she tightened her hold on his hand. "Not always," she corrected softly. "For a while I wore my heart on my sleeve."

"And then?"

Patience drew a deep breath and adapted the I-can-handle-anything attitude he so admired. "I realized, about a year after my parents' death, that the guys in the family were really counting on me to hold it together. So I began acting a lot braver than I felt and giving out advice on everything under the sun to kind of prove I knew what I was doing. Before long, I felt like I was absolutely in control. And my confidence grew."

"Enough to get you into Yale," Josh recalled.

"Yes."

"Max was proud of that, too. You were the first and only McKendrick to go Ivy League."

Patience's expression grew wistful, as did her tone. "I just wish he were here to see me take on the challenges of parenthood, too. He would have made a great granduncle."

Josh thought so, too. He hadn't expected it when he arrived at the Silver Spur, but he'd gotten close to Max, too. He would miss him. He took a moment to get a handle on his emotions, then said, "Speaking of Max . . . how do you think his plans for us are going so far?"

AT THE MENTION of her uncle's matchmaking, some of the levity returned to Patience's blue eyes. "You mean aside from the fact my cat Tweedles—who could deliver any day—has disappeared, your dog Goldie is in heat and hopelessly lovesick for Wrangler, and you and I are stuck together like glue until the wedding?" she recited, wrinkling her nose at him playfully.

To her mounting pleasure, Josh wrapped his hands around her waist and tugged her near. "Aside from all that," he said in a low, sexy voice rife with amusement.

"Aside from all that, we're doing fine," Patience remarked, splaying her hands caressingly across his chest.

"My findings exactly," Josh said meaningfully. And just that simply, he crushed her against him in a long, hot, searingly possessive kiss. She gave him back everything he expected, everything he wanted. Her lips pressed against his, her kisses whisper-soft at first, then ever more aggressive until the pleasure was sharp, stunning.

Patience hadn't expected him to kiss her again, but she was glad he had. Overwhelmed, she clung to him and kissed him back until she didn't want to think, until she wanted only to lose herself in the strength of his arms and the seducing tenderness of his kiss. Her hands crept up his chest to link around his neck as his hands kneaded their way seductively down her back.

With a groan of pleasure, she tangled her fingers in his hair and dragged him closer yet. It had been such a long long time since she'd felt this way. If she had ever felt this way. And still the sultry kiss continued, until they were trembling and straining toward each other, until it became apparent they had a decision to make.

Finally, he lifted his head so their eyes met. Even through the haze of passion, she could see the depth of his desire, the fierce determination to have her in his bed. Not just once. But again and again. She knew once made, the step taken, the decision would be irrevocable. There would be no backing up. No going back to being just on the verge of being friends. And though she readily admitted she wanted to be a lot more than friends with Josh, was she ready for anything more at this point? Never mind such a gargantuan step!

"What was that for?" Patience asked breathlessly, figuring, if nothing else, she could stall for a little time to figure things out.

His glance unexpectedly affectionate and unrepentantly sensual, Josh tucked a strand of silky hair behind her ear. Leaning closer, he touched his mouth to hers and tangled both his hands in her hair. "For being a good sport. You could have made us both miserable for the duration of our engagement, you could have ruthlessly used me to gain what should by all rights be yours even without Max's eccentric demands, and you haven't done either. I think that deserved a simple thank-you, and that," he said, a little more huskily than she sensed he intended, "was it."

She didn't want to see the adoration in his eyes. Didn't want to fall prey to her Uncle Max's plans, because that was just too easy, and she had learned the hard way that life was never that easy. When it was, something was bound to go wrong. Swiftly. Tempted to surrender to the desire they were both feeling anyway, she rested her hands on his chest and pushed away from him. "Don't get too cocky, Josh," she warned seriously. "Our betrothal is young yet." There was still so much that could happen...and that scared her, so much.

"And yet we're getting on." He brought her close again, their bodies melding together effortlessly, touching in one electrified line. "So much so that..." He cut himself short, abruptly looking as if he'd said too much.

"What?" Patience prodded. Dangerous or not, she needed to know what he was feeling and thinking every step of the way. It was the only way either of them would survive such a crazy situation with their hearts intact.

Gently, he cupped her chin in his hand. "Has it occurred to you that maybe Max was right?" he asked in a soft, serious voice. "That maybe we should throw caution to the wind and have a child together?"

Chapter Six

Dear Patience,
Should I marry my boyfriend just because we
want to have a baby together? He says it's not
necessary. What do you think?

Signed,
Unsure About Matrimony

Dear Unsure About Matrimony,
In this instance, two parents are better than one.
Lasso that beau and reel him in.

Rootin' for You,
Patience

Patience stared at Josh in stunned amazement, her lack
of an immediate comeback showing a weakness for the
idea that she could only pray he hadn't noticed. "Making babies with me was not a part of your job description, Josh."

His sensual lips curved in a slow, seductive smile.
"But it is part of Max's will."

Needing some physical space if she was going to be
able to think clearly, Patience stepped out of the warm
circle of Josh's embrace. She folded her arms beneath

her breasts. "I loved my uncle dearly, but Max was pushing it, even bringing that up."

He remained cavalierly unperturbed. "Still, the subject has been broached."

"And you're willing." She didn't know whether to laugh or exult at the unexpected turn her life was taking; she just knew she felt as if she'd hopped on a carousel of fortune—good and bad—that would not stop.

"I would like to have a child. Like you, I'm not getting any younger. Like you, I have yet to find a mate to settle down with."

"Nor are we sure, at this point, that you can stay in one place," Patience pointed out coolly, knowing the one thing she could not bear was to be left in the lurch again by the man she loved.

He gave her a slow, unsettling smile that set her pulse to racing. "I could. With the right motivation."

"The right motivation being a child," Patience guessed.

"And a wife," he added with a resolute glance, letting her know that for him there was no other way. It would be all or nothing.

His proposition sounded good on the surface, but Patience knew there was much to consider. "You should love the person you marry, Josh." *We both should.*

"Or grow to love her," he corrected quietly. In his view, they were the same thing.

Patience drew a quick breath. She knew they were under a time limit here, but he was moving too fast, pushing too hard. "We're headed into dangerous territory here, Josh." She started to turn away.

Hands on her shoulders, he pulled her right back. His pewter eyes narrowed on hers. "Not as dangerous as I'd like. I meant what I said. I want a child with you, Patience.''

Patience broke away from him and headed toward the house. ''Just like that?''

Hands shoved in the pockets of his jeans, his steps long and leisurely, he accompanied her toward the log cabin. ''I've wanted a family for a long time.''

Patience's shoes smacked the driveway with every step. She headed up the steps and back inside the house. ''Have there been other women in your life?''

Josh shut the door behind them, closing out the outside world. ''Only one who meant a lot to me, and that was a long time ago.''

Unwilling to go back upstairs to the bedroom, Patience sank onto one of the cranberry red sofas in front of the fireplace and asked a question she had a gut feeling was not likely to be well received. ''What happened to break you up?''

SHE WAS ASKING QUESTIONS Josh did not want to answer, yet knew he must. His expression both diffident and evasive, he replied, ''It was a lot of things.''

''I'm listening.''

That was the problem. He knew she was. Too well, as a matter of fact. Feigning an indifference he couldn't begin to feel, he shrugged. ''In some ways I didn't move fast enough, in other ways I moved too fast.''

''In what ways?'' Patience persisted.

Josh's jaw tensed as it always did when he found himself faced with questions he could not answer, not completely anyway. Finally he said, as truthfully as he could, ''I knew my father was not likely to approve of the match when he learned the woman I loved was wealthy.''

Patience went very still. He knew she was mentally comparing his romantic past with their current situation. "But you got involved anyway," she guessed.

Josh shrugged in remembered frustration. Back then, he had taken so much for granted. No more. "I didn't think dollars and cents should matter. Still—" he scowled, silently berating himself for what had later turned out to be crucial mistakes on his part "—I should have tried to talk some sense into my dad a lot sooner."

Patience watched him restlessly prowl the room. "I gather you weren't successful when you did try."

Josh stiffened. "No. I wasn't. But it was more than that. If I had just been paying attention to everything that was going on at the time, I can't help but think that maybe I could have prevented the hardships and heartaches that followed." He could have prevented the end of that awful night, which even now, after all this time, memory couldn't erase.

HE CAME TO SLOWLY, every inch of him wet and broken and aching with pain unlike anything he had ever known. Groaning, he tried to lift his head to look around and get his bearings, but the effort proved too much, and once again he landed facedown in the dirt.

Panting hard, he lay very still, acclimatizing himself to his surroundings, and gathered the strength to try again. Somehow, he had been thrown free of the car. He had landed in the ravine beneath the cliff, some distance away from the mangled vehicle. Broken bones or no, he knew he had to get out of there. He knew he was in danger, as was his companion. And it wasn't just from the thugs, who might still be in the area, waiting to gloat over a job well-done. Already, the pungent smell of gasoline and the warning smell of smoke filled his nostrils. They had the cover of night, but for how long? he wondered, desperate to get out of there.

Trying again, he levered himself up on his elbows just as the first flash of fire burst from the car and lit up the sky. The boom that followed shook the earth.

"No!" he shouted hoarsely as debris rained down on him and he took in the shadowy figure still trapped behind the wheel of the burning car. "God, no..."

"I DON'T UNDERSTAND." Patience's voice brought Josh out of his painful reverie and back to the present. "Why do you feel so responsible?"

Josh turned back to her, his mood as harsh and self-indicting as his memories. "I was young and caught up in myself and my own problems. I wasn't paying attention to the events that were unfolding around me." He drew a grimly chastising breath, knowing, despite Patience's obvious opinion to the contrary, that he was not being too hard on himself. "As a consequence, I ended up losing both the woman I loved and my family at the same time. I don't intend for that to happen again." He would die before it happened again.

"So you've been alone all this time?"

"Yes, more or less. I've got friends. People I work with. But it's not the same as having family."

"And you've had no other chance to replace the family you lost?"

Josh shrugged and, knowing it was truer than Patience could ever realize, admitted, "I haven't had much to offer a woman."

"Now, that I find really hard to believe," Patience said. "I mean, it's obvious Uncle Max thought you were absolutely everything a woman could want in a potential father. Otherwise, he wouldn't have named you in his will.''

Josh shook his head in disbelief. Though he and Max had gotten along great, he could still hardly believe that had happened. Unless it was fate. He knew he wanted to be here. He wanted to see her smile. He wanted to be close enough to see the sparkle in her blue eyes. He wanted to be close enough to kiss and touch her every day. ''I think the question is, Patience, What do you think about my potential as a prospective father for your child?''

He tensed hopefully as he waited for her reply, knowing that so much—everything, it seemed—hinged on her wanting him, too.

''Well—''

To his surprise, Patience blushed a little and shyly glanced away. She stood and led the way almost too languorously into the adjacent kitchen. ''You are smart, and strong, and, well—there's really no other way to say it—handsome as sin.''

Josh hadn't expected her to list off his physical attributes like a customer choosing a stud. He would've preferred she concentrate on more important components to the marriage and parenthood equation, such as compatibility, shared values and the all-important chemistry flowing between the two of them. Nevertheless, the depth of her praise, the genuineness of his appeal to her, at least on a physical level, brought an answering warmth to his chest. ''Does that mean you'll think about it?'' Josh asked, amazed but pleased at the astonishingly good way things were working out. He had to hand it to Max. He really had known what he was doing, pairing them together in such an unusual way.

"I'll go you one better," Patience stipulated firmly. "I'll agree to it, but only on one condition."

DESPITE HER FIERCE DESIRE for a baby of her own, Josh hadn't expected convincing Patience to be this easy. And that had him on the lookout for the next pitfall. "What condition?" he asked as Patience turned out the lights in the kitchen, made sure the back door was locked, went back out into the hall and led the way upstairs. "That we make the baby the modern way."

Josh did not like the sound of that. It conjured up visions of chilly examining rooms and high-tech paraphernalia. Not candlelight and a warm bed and an abundance of romance.

Unable to help himself, he watched the unconsciously evocative play of her hips beneath the slender silk trousers. It was all he could do not to groan out loud in frustration. "You're not suggesting we do this via test tube, in some hospital?"

Patience turned to smile at him as she reached the top of the stairs. "Or via artificial insemination? Yes, that is exactly what I am suggesting. And I might add, under the conditions of our engagement to be married, it is all you should expect, Josh."

This was one possibility Josh didn't even have to think about. He followed her into the bedroom and sat down on the rumpled covers of the bed. "No way."

Patience snatched something pink and soft-looking out of her suitcase. "Why not?" she called over her shoulder, moving by him in a cloud of fragrance and disappearing into the adjacent bathroom.

Because I've felt the way you kiss me, the way you respond, and I know you want me as much as I want you, and making love to you would be a long-held dream come true.

"If I make a baby with you, Patience, I want it made the old-fashioned way," he qualified firmly.

Patience came back out of the bathroom, clad in a pair of pink thermal-knit pajamas that were, he expected, meant to be chaste but were even more sexy than the silk lounging outfit she'd had on minutes earlier. The pants were cut legging style—and clung to her slender thighs, hips and calves like a second skin. The tunic top was long—it came to just below her hips—clinging enough to mold the soft swell of her breasts and the nip of her waist, yet loose enough for a man to get his hands under without unfastening the row of buttons that went all the way down the front. And Josh found he very much wanted to get his hands beneath that soft-looking shirt and on the even softer expanse of her fair satin skin.

"No way, Josh. No way in hell am I doing that!" Patience stormed.

Josh stood and moved around, hoping that would ease the constriction at the front of his jeans. "Why not?" Deciding it was too hot in there to sleep with so many damn clothes on, he took off his chambray shirt and tossed it onto the dresser top.

Her mouth dropped into a round O of surprise and her cheeks flushed a very becoming pink. Looking as if she were struggling to keep her mind on the argument they were having, she said, "Because doing it that way puts a whole different spin on the situation."

Josh shrugged. He took off his belt and socks, but because he had no pajamas, he reluctantly left on his jeans. "It probably would bring us closer together." He drew back the covers on his side of the bed to reveal the cool, crisp sheets beneath and lay back on the pillow, his hands folded behind his head.

Patience snapped off the light and crawled beneath the covers on her own side, swiftly drawing them up to her chin. "I don't want to be that close to you."

Liar, Josh thought, and it was all he could do not to draw her into his arms and kiss her again. Only the thought he would not want to stop kept him from doing so. He didn't want to scare her off. And he knew making love to her would frighten her, much more than the kisses they'd exchanged earlier.

Silence reigned between them.

He listened to the rapid rise and fall of her breath, saw the genuine panic on her face and suddenly knew Patience was as scared of herself and her own feelings as she was of him. "You don't want to be that close to anyone again, do you?" he asked softly.

"Not at the moment, no," Patience said stiffly, rolling onto her side and putting her pillow, like a shield, directly between them.

"You know what they say," he taunted, rolling onto his side so they were stretched out length to length, facing each other. "Nothing ventured, nothing lost!" He reached out and ran his hand down her face, wishing he could kiss her again, wishing he could have all of her, heart and soul. "And you, Patience McKendrick, haven't taken any real risks in a long time."

Patience waited until he dropped his hand, then blew out an irritated breath. "Like you have, Mr. I-Was-Only-Serious-About-A-Woman-Once," she grumbled back.

Josh grinned. He hadn't planned any of this, but it was easy to see he was getting under her skin. He liked the feeling. "So I've been busy," he fibbed, knowing that was only a small part of why he hadn't been involved with anyone.

Patience's delectably soft lower lip slid out into an appealing pout. "So have I."

"But I didn't say I wasn't looking," Josh continued affably, watching the moonlight play over her hair and skin, knowing that even if things didn't work out, he would always have the memories of this night, of being close to her again.

Patience drew a slightly calmer breath. "I was looking, too," she said.

Josh was glad she hadn't found anyone.

"There was just no one I met who had that special chemistry."

"Like the kind you and I have," Josh observed as a dizzying excitement raced through him, arousing him further.

Patience rolled so her back was to him and left her pillow wedged between them. "Chemistry isn't the only thing necessary to make a marriage last, Josh," she replied sternly between soft, jerky breaths.

"But it's a start," Josh replied, and was pleased when she had no answer to that.

31:00

OBLIVIOUS TO THE MORNING sunshine streaming in through her studio windows, Patience stared at the glowing letters on her computer screen. It used to be that she answered as many letters on how to deal with one's in-laws, children and nosy neighbors as spouses, mates and dates, she thought as she cradled a steaming mug of coffee in her hands. But lately... Was it her imagination, or were all these letters beginning to have a common theme? Love. More to the point, was anyone out there not searching for love? Including herself.

Shaking her head, she sipped her coffee and turned her attention back to the letter she was trying to answer and read it again.

Dear Patience,
Is it true? Do opposites really attract?

Sincerely,
Magnetic Miss

Patience studied the letter a while longer, mentally formulating her answer, then put her mug aside and began to type.

Dear Magnetic Miss,
Only if you're interested in an I've-been-ridden-roughshod relationship.

Only, she thought, if you're interested in embarking on something faintly dangerous and very exciting, like my relationship with Josh Colter....

"I don't know, Patience," a deep voice intoned over her shoulder, making her jump. "That advice sounds a little bit cut-and-dried to me. Maybe a little overly cautious, too."

Patience caught a whiff of English Leather cologne and glanced up to see Josh standing beside her. A mug of coffee cradled in his hands, he was reading what she had just typed on the computer screen.

"I think mixing fire and ice can be a great thing," Josh continued lazily, taking a seat on the edge of her desk and folding his arms in front of him.

Patience tried not to think how glad she was to see him. Which was odd, because she had been ticked off at him when she finally went to sleep for his we-can-do-this-the-old-fashioned-way-if-we-only-want-to attitude toward baby making. "You're speaking from experience, I gather."

Showing no outward sign of the restless night they had both had, he shrugged and gently tugged at a lock of her hair. "It never hurts to do a little experimentin'."

Her heart racing but her outward demeanor cool, Patience pushed away from the desk. "On me?" she asked, preferring to confront him from a physically superior position.

Looking every inch the mischievous cowboy, Josh shrugged. "If the shoe fits..." Lacing his hands around her waist, he shifted her between the open vee of his legs and pulled her down onto his lap. "Besides," he murmured as he stared down at her and traced her lips with the pad of his thumb, "I think you need me to shake up your dull, safe world. That's why Max linked the two of us together."

Patience lifted a dissenting eyebrow, trying not to let him know how he was affecting her. "And that's what you intend to do, no doubt?"

"I aim to please." Josh bent and pressed an all-too-brief, all-too-casual kiss to her lips.

"Always have, always will. Now back to your writing." He held her against him gently. "It's been sounding a bit too world-weary, don't you think?"

She had just been thinking the same thing, but hearing it from him irritated her. Using her hands as leverage, she vaulted off his lap and away from him. "The tart-tongued, cynical approach is what my readers want from me, Josh. They want me to be that inner voice that alerts them to the dangers ahead and keeps them from making foolhardy mistakes that have the potential to ruin their lives."

"Now you're really sounding cynical," he teased.

With chagrin, Patience realized that was so, but she couldn't seem to help it. "Life has a way of doing that to you," she retorted, deliberately keeping her tone flip, "and I admit I am more cautious these days than I was in my wild youth. Not that you're one to talk, Josh Colter." She leveled a lecturing finger his way. "I don't see you with particularly close ties to those around you."

Josh's expression changed. He became abruptly remote, unhappy. "Like you said, life has a way of getting in the way sometimes."

As do old romances, Patience thought, watching as he rose and swaggered off.

She joined him in the kitchen for breakfast. "Tell me more about this woman you were in love with once," she said as he poured cold cereal into a bowl.

Josh frowned, not particularly excited about cooperating with her request. "What do you want to know?" he asked gruffly.

Why just the mention of her upsets you, for one thing, Patience thought. Having already eaten cereal upon rising, she contented herself with another cup of coffee. "Are you still in love with her?"

Josh ate his cereal with more than necessary concentration.

"You don't want to answer that, do you?" Patience guessed.

He shrugged uncaringly. "I don't see the point."

"You're avoiding the question."

"Okay." He sat back in his chair. "I guess a part of me is still in love with her and always will be."

Patience was crushed by that. She tried to keep her feelings to herself. "Is there a chance the two of you will ever get back together?"

Another pause. Even longer. As if Josh just couldn't decide what to say to that. "No," he said finally, looking even more irritated.

"Why not?" Patience asked curiously.

"Because there are some things in life that can't be reconstructed." He went back to eating his cereal with single-minded concentration.

Patience studied him over the rim of her coffee cup. He seemed curiously resigned to that for so fearless and ambitious a person. "Have you tried?"

Josh's mouth tightened. "There was no point in trying to go back," he said flatly. "I was young and very involved with my own problems at the time and I didn't treat her fairly. She had no reason to want to reconcile with me, then or ever."

He sounded so definite about it. He sounded as if he were still half in love with this mystery woman, Patience thought, disappointed. Or at the very least not really over her, not the way she was starting to get over Alec, anyway. "Maybe if you went to her and told her you had changed," Patience suggested after a moment, feeling a little stunned at how much Josh was holding back from her.

"No." Josh finished his cereal. He carried his bowl to the sink, then returned to her side. Reaching down, he captured her hand and brought her to her feet. Both hands landed on her waist. He looked down at her, his gaze as blunt and implacable as his low words. "I am not interested in resurrecting the past, Patience. I want a future. I want to start fresh. The question is—" he paused, sliding his hands through her hair and tilting her face up to his "—are you willing to do the same?"

Was she?

Ten seconds later, Patience still didn't know.

"That's a heck of a question to be asking someone you've just met," Patience said softly.

His eyes never wavered. "Nevertheless, it's a fair one," he retorted softly, his gaze first tracing, then lingering on her lips. "Besides, Max didn't give us much choice. He wanted us joined at the hip so we could quickly get questions like this out of the way. So what's your answer, Patience?" he persisted doggedly. "Will you or won't you give me a chance?"

JOSH WAITED FOR PATIENCE to reply, knowing the one thing he had never expected or wanted from her was an easy capitulation.

"You know how to take a woman's breath away, I'll grant you that," she replied finally, as even more color flooded into her cheeks.

"I've learned to go after what I want," Josh replied simply, and it was true. These days, nothing and no one stood in his way. When it came to surviving, he was ready and willing to do whatever it took. He sensed that Patience—though she had yet to be as thoroughly tested as he had been—was, too.

"And what you want is a baby," she said.

More than she could ever know, Josh thought. "A baby and you," he replied, wanting there to be no mistake about that.

"And a home here on the Silver Spur."

"That is what Max and I talked about. I just had no idea it would be as your husband."

"But making your home here appealed to you?" Patience ascertained.

"Yes, it did," Josh admitted freely. Initially, he'd felt it would be enough to be here on the ranch and see Patience on her holiday visits. Initially, he'd thought it would be enough just to know she was okay.

But now, having spent time with her one-on-one, he wanted more. He wanted to see her and talk with her, hold her and make love to her as if there were no tomorrow. Marrying her, as Max had obviously wanted, was even better.

Unfortunately, the heartbreak of the past had robbed Patience of the impulsiveness he recalled and left her almost overly cautious. Josh studied her thoughtful, wary expression and felt as if he was trying to capture a firefly who simply wouldn't light but kept anxiously flitting from place to place. "You think I'm doing this because of the money, don't you?" he guessed unhappily.

Patience went to the kitchen sink. Turning so her back was to him, she poured the rest of her coffee down the drain. "You can't tell me dollars and cents don't figure into it," she said flatly. "If they didn't, neither of us would be here now."

Crossing the distance between them, Josh put his hands on her shoulders and turned her so she had to face him. "I would have honored anything Max had asked me to do in his will," he vowed in a low voice, rife with respect. "I owe him that."

"So do I. But the money we both stand to gain from this inheritance colors things," Patience replied, troubled.

Josh shook his head. "It doesn't have to. Hell, if you want, if it's going to pose a problem between us, we could voluntarily give it up." He would gladly sacrifice the ranch for a life with Patience.

Patience bit her lower lip indecisively. "Max wouldn't have wanted that, either, Josh. He wanted the Silver Spur Ranch to stay in the family."

Feeling she might bolt at any moment, Josh tightened his hands on her shoulders. The possessiveness he felt for this woman still astounded him. "Then we follow through."

Patience wrapped her arms around his waist and sagged against him. "Oh, Josh. You make it sound so easy."

He stroked her hair gently. "It could be, Patience, if we let it be."

She shook her head in silent consternation, looking as if this really were too much to discuss, and he knew, once again, he was pushing too hard, too fast.

FEARING SHE WAS EMBARKING on the same kind of whirlwind romance she had embarked on with Alec, Patience decided it was time to pull back a little, regroup and figure out if this was really the direction she wanted her life to go. Stepping out of the warm, inviting circle of Josh's arms, she tipped her face up to his and said briskly, "I really have to get back to my column, finish it and fax it in before the Sunday edition deadline."

Looking abruptly regretful they had shared so much, too, Josh accepted her decision with a nod, adding, "I've got to update the medical records on the new stallions. I can work in the living room. The files are already here. I had them brought along with Goldie."

Without Josh around to distract her, Patience finished her letters to her readers in short order and faxed them in. She bypassed him quietly and went out to the kitchen to get another cup of coffee and see if they needed anything from the supermarket.

Opening the cupboards to check out the contents, she came across an electric baby food warmer, several baby bottles and a stack of washable bibs. Again, there was a little note from Uncle Max. It said, "Nothing would make me happier than to see you with a young'un running around."

Patience smiled and leaned against the counter. What would it be like, she wondered, getting up every morning to fix breakfast for her husband and child? To have a high chair at the table? To have her day brightened by their baby's smiles? If the baby was a boy, would he look like Josh? Would he have his eyes or hers?

And what kind of daddy would he be? Gentle, that went without saying. Probably fiercely protective, too.

She could imagine Josh tenderly cuddling their baby against his chest. Or playing with the baby. Coaxing the little one to talk. And laugh out loud and smile.

He would be there as much as she would let him be. The question was, Did she want Josh in her bed and her life, not just temporarily, but for the decades it took to bring up a child? Judging by the way he set things up in his will, Max had seemed to think it was a good idea. Which meant Max approved of Josh to the nth degree.

Patience sighed, wishing that Max had felt that way about her and Alec, yet recalling all too well how different his attitude had been, and how it had colored her relationship with Alec.

She thought back to the night they'd set a wedding date, and the chain of events that had precipitated it.

Alec had known she was upset the moment she walked in his dorm room that cold January night.

"*WHAT'S WRONG?*" *he asked.*

"*Everything!*" *Patience stepped over the books, papers and magazines he'd piled every which way, flung off her coat and tossed it down on the unmade covers of his bed. One of the things she liked best about Alec was that he was as hopelessly messy as she was. Perfectly comfortable in the chaos of his room, she swung back around to face him. "Uncle Max not only refuses to give us his blessing, he refuses to attend our wedding on Valentine's Day!" She didn't bother to hide the tears streaming down her face. She had never felt so hurt or so angry in her life.*

Alec rummaged around his desk. Failing to find any tissues, he wiped her face with the corner of a just washed towel, still warm from the dorm clothes dryer. When he had finished, he threw the towel aside and pulled her into his arms, stroking her hair all the while. "I was afraid he'd feel this way," he murmured, gently pressing a kiss to her temple.

With effort, Patience pulled herself together. "Did you tell your father?"

Alec stiffened and for a long moment said nothing. Patience drew back slightly to better see his face. Alec stared past her, his jaw set, his glasses sliding down on the end of his nose. "He's not going to come, either."

Patience let her head fall forward until it rested against Alec's chest. "This is such a mess."

Alec sighed. "Maybe we should wait."

"*No,*" *Patience said stubbornly. "I want to get married now. Just like we planned. And we will, Alec. We'll throw ourselves a wedding with the trust fund money my parents left me. It's not all that much, granted, but it's enough to buy us the wedding of our dreams."*

Alec paused, his expression troubled, as he ran a hand through his short blond hair. "You're sure this is what you want?"

Patience nodded determinedly, ignoring the doubts she saw on his face. She was sure enough for both of them....

LOOKING BACK on her engagement, though, Patience had to wonder. Had she given Alec a chance to rescind his proposal? Or had the rush to marry been more one-sided than she knew? Had Alec secretly wanted to back out by then, and just been afraid to say so for fear of hurting her feelings?

Was she making a similar mistake with Josh in even thinking of honoring Max's wishes?

She knew he desired her, just as Alec had.

She knew from the way he looked at her sometimes when he thought she wasn't aware of it that he might even come to love her one day.

But she also knew that Josh was restless in a way that Alec hadn't been. And that restlessness of his could end up spelling trouble for them both, she worried. Because she couldn't bear it if he walked out on her one day, the way Alec had.

Just then the phone began to ring. Thinking it might be her editor, with some comment on the letters she had just faxed in for the Sunday edition, Patience reached for the phone. "I'll get it," she called to Josh before he could pick up the extension in there.

As it turned out, it was a woman on the other end, all right. But the call was not for Patience.

"Just a moment, I'll get him," she said as Josh walked into the kitchen. She handed the phone over to him. "Holly Diehl wants to talk to you."

Chapter Seven

Dear Patience,
My fiancé says a little mystery is good for the relationship. Is he right?

Sincerely,
No Nancy Drew

Dear No Nancy Drew,
Mystery in a relationship is only good for Mata
Hari. Know everything or move on to the next
trail. Take nothing on faith alone.

Looking Out for You,
Patience

29:02

Patience watched Josh's face as he talked on the phone
in clipped answers of "yes," "no," and "I'll have to get
back to you on that." Finally, about two minutes into
the conversation, he advised Holly to consult Soaring
Eagle concerning any questions she might have about
training a new foal, since he was the head trainer on the
ranch. He said a rather terse goodbye and hung up the
phone. It was pretty clear to Patience that the call from
Holly had been as much of a personal as professional

nature. It was also clear Josh would have preferred she not overhear any of it.

"Problem?" Patience asked, still wondering what exactly Josh's relationship with Holly Diehl was.

Josh shook his head. "No. She just had a few questions. I told her what she needed to know on the phone. I need to go into town to do a few errands. What would you think about going with me and having lunch there, at Pearl's Diner?"

"Sounds good to me," Patience said. It would give her a chance to drop by Cisco Kidd's office and find out what was up with his investigation of Josh. If he hadn't come up with anything so far, she just might ask him to call it off. The truth was, she was beginning to feel a little guilty about even having ordered it. It wasn't like her to investigate someone behind his or her back. It was just this situation that Max had initiated that had her thinking and doing so many crazy things, had her feeling that there was something she should know or notice or recall, hovering just beyond her consciousness....

"I've got some errands to do, too," she finished brightly.

An hour later, they were sitting in a booth at Pearl's.

"Don't the two of you look cozy," Pearl said as she put plates of steaming chicken tetrazzini in front of Josh and Patience. "If Max gets his wish, there are going to be some beautiful babies being made on the Silver Spur."

Patience successfully struggled to contain a blush as she fibbed, "The only babies I am interested in at the moment are those due to be born to my Persian cat, Tweedles."

"When is she due?" Pearl asked, collecting their empty salad plates.

"Any day."

"Problem is," Josh told Pearl, "Tweedles has disappeared."

"I haven't seen her in a good twenty hours now," Patience told Pearl as she topped off their glasses of iced tea. "And neither have any of the hired hands."

"She may have run off somewhere to have her babies in peace," Josh explained.

"Oh dear," Pearl said, setting the glass pitcher down with a thud. "Is that safe on a sprawling ranch like the Silver Spur?"

"It worries me, too," Patience admitted freely. "There's a lot of wildlife out there, not all of it friendly. And Tweedles is very much a city cat."

"Don't worry. We'll find her," Josh said. And looking into his eyes, she could believe he meant it. "Maybe not before she delivers, but someone will stumble across her, I'm sure. She may be lying low but she probably didn't go too far from the house. There are too many hired hands for someone not to see something eventually."

"Well, good luck to you on both scores," Pearl replied, her eyes looking a little moist. "I know more than anything Max wanted you both to be happy."

"That's the problem," Patience said as Pearl moved off to attend to other customers and she and Josh dug in to their entrée. "I don't want any of this because it was what Max wanted. And yet there's a part of me that feels I should do exactly what he wanted as a way of honoring him and his last wishes."

"I know what you mean," Josh said. "I feel that way, too."

"But—?" Patience prodded, sensing there was more.

"Bottom line. I'm still willing to marry you so you can inherit. But I'm not making babies . . . I'm not going to make ours a real marriage . . . just because of his will."

"Nor will I," Patience agreed wholeheartedly. Yet more and more it was beginning to seem like a real possibility. For the first time in years, real happiness and the family she had always wanted seemed within her grasp.

Josh smiled. He seemed pleased with her reaction as he reached across the table and took her hand. "If it happens," he said in a low, serious voice, "I want you to know it'll be because the time and circumstances are right for both of us."

"DID YOU HAVE ANY TROUBLE slipping away to see me?" Cisco asked Patience half an hour later.

"None," she reported as she slipped into a chair in front of Cisco's desk. Although, she amended silently, she felt guilty as heck for lying to Josh about what she was going to do. He thought she was off buying some cosmetics. "We were due to take our thirty-minute breaks apart sometime, and this is our first."

"Does Josh know you're here?"

"Not exactly." Her conscience still prickling unbearably, Patience put her purse down next to her feet. "I sort of took off in the direction of the drugstore, then slipped around to your office through the back alley."

"What's he doing right now?"

"He had some errands, too. So, what have you come up with on Josh so far?" Patience was fervently hoping it was nothing.

"So far his background and the employment history you gave me on him check out exactly. There's not a glitch in his history, not even a parking ticket so far as I can tell. In some ways it was almost too perfect for a rough-around-the-edges guy like Josh."

"My thoughts exactly. I mean, his face has those tiny scars on it, a couple above his eyebrow, another just below his lip, and his nose looks like it's been broken—but never reset—too. All that, coupled with the don't-mess-with-me way he carries himself, adds up to a guy who has not only been around but seen a barroom fight or two."

"Yet those in barroom brawls or street fights usually get arrested," Cisco returned evenly, turning the gold pen in his hand end over end. "And Josh Colter has no record of arrests."

"That's good, isn't it?" Patience asked. Except for the fact that his squeaky-clean but very restless past made her wonder all the more.

Cisco made a seesawing motion with his hand. Patience had never seen him look more serious. "To be straight with you, Patience, I don't know if it's good or bad. It could be that Josh has no criminal record and we're letting our imaginations run away with us. On the other hand, he could be from a background that is every bit as rough-and-tumble as we think."

"Then why wouldn't it show up?"

Cisco laid down his pen but did not immediately share his thoughts with her. "Maybe he has friends in high places who could help erase whatever troubles Josh had in his misspent youth," Cisco suggested finally.

"Friends like Max," Patience assumed slowly.

Cisco nodded.

Patience was silent. She knew, although it was one of those things that was never discussed, that Max had done much the same thing for Cisco years and years ago.

She didn't know what kind of trouble a teenage Cisco had been in, only that Max had helped extricate him from it. And that the subject had never since been discussed. The problems in Cisco's past had been sufficiently wiped out to allow him to turn his life around, attend college and law school and join the bar. In return, Max had welcomed Cisco's deep loyalty to him and made him his attorney. He had also confided in Cisco many things. As a result, Cisco and Max had become very close.

Was it possible Max had done the same for Josh, Patience wondered, by taking him under his wing and giving him a job? And that this was one of the reasons Josh felt beholden to Max? And was he agreeing to marry her, perhaps even sire a child for her, out of that same sense of indebtedness? Or was something else motivating Josh to go along with this crazy marriage of convenience and baby-making idea? Something neither she nor Cisco was seeing?

"Do you want me to keep looking?" Cisco asked.

Patience shook her head adamantly. "No. I have the feeling that whatever Josh is hiding from me is not in any official documents or files." Her gut feeling was that Max or Josh—or both—would have seen to that.

"You doing okay otherwise?" Cisco asked.

Patience nodded. And it was true, if you discounted the fact she was falling hard for a man she wasn't even quite sure she could trust any more than she had been able to trust Alec Vaughn. But that was not something

Cisco or anyone else could help her with. She would just have to figure that out for herself.

Knowing she had taken up far too much of Cisco's time, and her thirty minutes apart from Josh were about up, Patience stood. "Thanks for checking Josh out," she told Cisco. She felt sort of relieved.

"No problem. I'm always here for you."

Patience headed out the same way she had come in, via the back route. She was shocked to see she wasn't the only one who had selected the alley as a path. Josh was deep in conversation with none other than Holly Diehl.

Before Patience could figure out what they were doing, or even attempt to decipher what was being said between the two of them in low, urgent whispers, Josh glanced up.

As their eyes clashed and held, Patience saw his shock. His remorse. His guilt. And knew he had not wanted her to find this out. Stunned with the depth of her hurt, furious at her own naïveté in believing Holly was only a client to Josh, Patience wheeled away. She had to get the heck out of there. Fast. Before she did or said something they would all regret.

PATIENCE WAS ALREADY behind the wheel of the Silver Spur pickup when Josh caught up with her. Apparently sensing correctly that she not only was prepared to leave without him but had been hoping that would be the case, he swung himself up and into the passenger seat.

Patience slammed into reverse, backed out of the angled parking space in front of Pearl's with a screech and slammed right back into drive. Josh's jaw was tense with anger, too, as she headed toward the ranch in silence, but the fervent explanations she expected from him never came.

Mile after mile of Montana grassland passed, and still no word, not so much as a sigh from Josh.

Finally she turned at the ranch road and headed up the drive to the house. Still nothing from Josh. And Patience found she had nothing to say to him, either. Her shoulders stiff with a combination of hurt and resignation, she parked and got out of the truck.

"I'm going to look in on the foals," Patience said.

"I'll go with you."

She was aware of Josh shadowing her as they threaded their way through the horse complex to the foaling barn. She was also aware she hadn't felt such a flood of emotion since Alec had jilted her years ago. Tears stinging her eyes, Patience wondered if she would ever stop making such a fool of herself over men. She certainly knew how to pick 'em, as Max would've said. The only problem, she thought bitterly, was that Max had picked this one, too.

To Patience's relief as they walked down the aisle, checking stall after stall, all the foals were nursing contentedly at their mothers' sides. Would she ever feel the same joy? she wondered miserably. Or was motherhood destined to elude her, too?

"At least some of us around here are doing well," she murmured beneath her breath. Figuring she had seen enough, and been with Josh long enough, she started to step past him.

Josh stepped with her, blocking her exit out of the barn. Capable hands braced on his hips, long legs planted combatively apart, he looked as if he'd had just about enough of the silent treatment from her. And for one fleeting moment, she wondered if she had erroneously jumped to conclusions. Then she flashed back to the guilt she had seen on his face when he was standing there with Holly Diehl, and she knew she hadn't misjudged anything. Something was going on there that he did not want her to know anything about.

"There's an explanation for what you just saw in town if you want to hear it," Josh began grimly.

Patience stiffened. "You don't owe me any explanation, Josh." *We're not married yet.* The way things were going, they were not even close to it anymore.

"Yeah, well, I think I do," he said reluctantly.

Patience angled her chin up at him, daring him to try to hoodwink her again. "I admit the possibility of you already being close to someone did not cross my mind until today," she told him coolly, as if this all were nothing to her. As if he were nothing to her. She drew a stabilizing breath. "But in retrospect I realize Max and I both were fools not to anticipate this." *Me especially. I should have known better.*

"Anticipate what?" he demanded tersely.

"Your involvement with Holly Diehl. Obviously, she is more than a run-of-the-mill horse owner to you."

Josh blew out an exasperated breath and shook his head in silent remonstration, which ended in a quick grimace. "Holly Diehl means nothing to me, Patience. Do you hear me? Nothing."

How could Holly mean anything when he associated her with one of the worst times of his life? Josh thought. When Holly had been a pivotal force in keeping him from the woman he had still loved with all his heart and soul....

"STOP IT, JOSH. You're not getting out of here," Holly Diehl had said the first time he had tried to leave.

"The hell I'm not." Fed up with the hiding and the lying, fed up with feeling like a damn prisoner in his own home, Josh strode for the door. Only to be cut off at the pass by a determined woman with a gun. *"You know you can't leave,"* Holly continued. *"Not until you finish what you started."*

Josh slammed his duffel bag onto the floor. *"I never agreed to all this."* Revenge, yes. Two long years of hell in hiding, no.

"You owe us, Josh. You owe him."

Josh fell silent. He had never said he did not want justice. He did. He burned for it, every hour and every minute of every night and day.

"You have to forget the past," Holly countered with the easy practicality he had come to hate. *"You have to move on."*

Josh felt the muscle in his jaw start up again. *"That's easy for you to say,"* he told Holly angrily. *"You didn't have to watch helplessly while those thugs beat the living daylights out of first him and then you. You didn't see your only family burn to death in that car. You didn't have to give up—"* Josh's voice caught in his throat at the thought of everything else he had, however inadvertently, lost. He shook his head, unable to go on. Wishing he could relive that time changed nothing. He knew that, and had for months now.

Holly touched his arm lightly. *"I know what you're thinking, but he put himself in that trap, Josh,"* she said gently, doing her best to soothe him with what she perceived was the truth. *"There was nothing you could have done to save him."*

Maybe and maybe not, Josh thought bitterly as he ran his hands through his hair. *"If only I'd paid attention. Noticed something, anything, sooner,"* he whispered, noting there was no end, and would never be an end, to his regret.

"And where would that have gotten you?" Holly challenged without empathy. "You were not equipped to deal with those men. We are. Face it, he did what he did. Just as you must now do what you have to do."

Josh turned away, his sense of failure and loss still acute.

"It's not as if there's anything left to go back to," Holly persuaded softly but firmly, laying a hand on his arm. "Like it or not, it's all gone, Josh. Everything."

"Meaning what?" Josh retorted angrily, shrugging off her touch. "I'm to be a rolling stone from this point forward?"

Holly shrugged and, predictably, offered not an ounce of sympathy. "It could be worse. You could be dead," she pointed out sagely.

In many ways, Josh thought, he already was.

"Maybe you're right," he said gruffly at last, knowing Holly was right, that he had no other options. "Maybe this is what I deserve." The loneliness he would feel the rest of his life would be a punishment for what he'd done. Not just to himself and the family he loved, but to Patience McKendrick. Beautiful, sweet, innocent, fiery Patience McKendrick.

Holly shook her head. "You're thinking of her again, aren't you?"

Josh refused to pretend otherwise. He swallowed around the lump in his throat and answered gruffly, "Knowing how she must feel about everything that's happened—what little she knows of it—it's hard not to think of her." His mood went from brooding to tortured in an instant. He gritted his teeth against the ache *in his heart. "Maybe it wasn't intentional, but the end result is that I've ruined her life and I've ruined mine."*

And for that, Josh had thought sadly then and now, he would always pay. . . .

"DOES HOLLY KNOW how you feel about her?" Patience persisted.

Josh folded his arms in front of him. He regarded her silently, refusing to disclose more. He had given away far too much as it was, just allowing himself to be seen with Holly. Yet with Patience hot on the heels of his past, how could he have done otherwise? he thought resentfully. He had to protect himself and her.

"I realize now what a quandary Max has put you in," Patience continued.

Josh focused on her hurt and bewilderment and it was all he could do not to take her in his arms. "That quandary being?" He took her rigid hand in his.

"The fact that you already have another woman in your life. I suppose it's natural for you to want the opportunity Max has afforded you by offering you half share in the horse-breeding operation. Not to worry. I have no intention of putting myself in a position where I could be jilted again, either before or after the marriage."

Sadness filled Josh, along with the frustration that he could never tell her everything. "I wouldn't jilt you, Patience," he said quietly.

Patience shook her head and laughed bitterly.

Josh's despair deepened. He tightened his grip on her fingers when she would have swept by him and tugged her back to his side. "You don't believe me, do you?"

Tears filled her eyes and rolled silently down her cheeks. But they did not alter the proud tilt of her head as she defiantly pried her fingers loose from his. "Alec once promised me he would never leave, either," she admitted in a low tone laced with bitter amusement. She lifted her eyes to his, every defense neatly back in place. "It was an empty promise." She drew a shaky breath and added stubbornly, "I am not opening myself up to that kind of hurt again."

Josh studied her upturned face and knew she meant it. But try as he might, he couldn't relive the past for her, fix things or make them right. Nor could he bring Alec back to her. "Is that why you were investigating me?" he inquired, feigning an inner tranquillity he couldn't begin to feel.

Patience went completely still. All the color drained from her face. "How did you know about that?" she demanded, trembling visibly.

"The McKendricks are not the only ones who have friends in high places. I'm capable of discovering things on the sly, too. As for the rest," he said, trapping her between the stall door and himself, "I am not involved with Holly Diehl, not in the way you think."

Josh watched as the blood drained from her face and her lips tightened. "So you said," Patience acknowledged in a low, jealous voice.

"She was a friend from my days at veterinarian school," Josh continued, telling as much of the truth as he could, while at the same time revealing nothing that would get either of them in any more trouble than they were already in. "She heard from mutual friends of ours that I was being checked out by Cisco Kidd on your behalf. That was why she called me this morning, from the guest quarters on the ranch, and why she insisted I meet with her in town, because she was leery of discussing what she had to say to me over the ranch phone system.''

Patience regarded him warily, as if she still sensed— damn correctly as it happened—that he wasn't telling her everything. Nor, suddenly, did she seem to care, and without warning, her eyes went all misty and romantic. As if she were as helplessly drawn to remembering the past as he was. And that could only mean even more trouble for them both, Josh knew. ''You're thinking about him again, aren't you?'' he demanded ruthlessly, wishing she would stop so they could both move on with their lives.

Though he sensed she knew exactly who he meant, she gave him a deliberately enigmatic look. ''Who?''

Josh did not want to play games. ''You know who,'' he retorted harshly, wondering what it was going to take to regain her trust again. ''Alec Vaughn.''

''So what if I am thinking of him?'' Her temper flared, reflecting in her eyes and her voice and her determined stance. She tossed her head, her pale, wheat blond hair flying like a silken halo about her face. ''Why should you be angry about that?''

''Because I am.''

''Why?'' she demanded in a careful tone that warned of simmering anger.

Josh braced an arm on the door beside her head and leaned in close, aware of Slim leading a horse just outside the other end of the barn, within earshot. ''It bothers me, all right?'' he murmured in her ear so only she could hear, then drew back so she could see deeply into his eyes. ''I don't want to see you hanging on to something that is over, especially when you know that Alec is not coming back, not ever.''

Patience bit her lip and he knew from the lingering sorrow in her eyes that she wasn't going to apologize for the love she still—and perhaps always would—carry somewhere deep inside her. "Knowing something is true in your head and feeling it in your heart are two different things," she murmured back, the hurt and loss she still felt thickening her voice.

Josh wanted to shake her. He wanted to say the hell with Slim and pull her all the way into his arms and comfort her, but he knew she wouldn't accept it. Fighting for control of his desire and the whims of his heart, he let out a long breath.

"You resent that, don't you?" she said softly.

She'd hurt him, but not the way she had intended, Josh thought. He backed away from her. "I resent the fact that you're deluding yourself," he replied with harsh authority, knowing he more than anyone else was an expert on that subject. He straightened and glowered down at her. "Alec is gone," he announced firmly. "And unless you can accept that, there is no future for us." Not waiting for her reply, he turned on his heel and stormed out.

JOSH WAS OUT IN THE YARD before Patience realized he had just initiated their second thirty-minute break apart. She didn't know if they should be taking it yet, since they still had more than twenty-four hours left before the wedding. She didn't know if they should try to stay together and save their breaks for later . . . when they might very well need them even more.

All she knew for certain was that she didn't want to use Josh to recapture the magic, mystery and excitement of her romantic past with Alec. And, she admitted to herself, in some strange way she had yet to completely figure out why she linked Josh with her time with Alec. They had the same explosive chemistry, the same quick intimacy. What they didn't have was trust. Or time. And as she watched him storm away from her furiously, she wasn't sure they ever would.

Muttering her frustration with him all the while, she headed out the opposite way, deciding now was as good a time as any to search for her missing cat, Tweedles. Around the paddocks she went. Past the corrals. Through the barn where the stallions were kept to the one containing the mares, past the bunkhouse and down around to the hay barn, where the feed was kept.

As Patience stepped inside, she became aware of how sunny and quiet it was in the hay barn. She tiptoed back through the various storage areas, then up the wooden stairs to the second floor, where she, Trace and Cody had sometimes played when they were kids.

There, in the back of the loft, was Tweedles, nestled in the hay. Surrounding her were six tiny Persian kittens, all nursing contentedly at their mama's side.

"So here you are," Patience whispered delightedly, sinking down into the hay beside her. "I've been looking all over for you. Don't you think it's time we got you and your babies back to the house?"

JOSH WATCHED PATIENCE dash off, realizing all too late he had just taken their second thirty-minute break apart. He swore heatedly as he continued storming across the yard. Normally he was, part by nature and part by choice, a very guarded man. Around Patience McKendrick, all that seemed to change. He found himself saying and doing things he had sworn he would never do. Worse, he didn't see that changing anytime soon. She pushed buttons in him that hadn't been pushed for years, buttons that had never been pushed before.

"Josh—thank heavens. I need to talk to you!"

He turned to see Holly Diehl standing just inside the hay barn. His lips thinned unhappily. Wasn't it enough that Holly and her cohorts had promised him the moon and instead ruined his life? Did they have to shadow his every move, too? He strode toward her, his anger growing by leaps and bounds. All he needed was for Patience to see him talking privately with Holly again and all hell would break loose.

"What are you doing here?" he demanded gruffly.

Holly, well used to his moods, remained unperturbed. She leaned against the barn door. Her smile was sunny and polite. "You know why I'm here, Josh. I came to finish the conversation we started in town."

Wary of being seen with the attractive brunette again, Josh grabbed her arm and ducked into the barn with her. "I asked you not to come back to the ranch!"

"I know," Holly said smoothly, "but I'm concerned about you, Josh."

As well you should be, Josh thought darkly. He gave his former housemate a warning look. "I did not ask for your constant attention."

Holly shrugged and gave him a stubborn smile. "Nevertheless, after all we went through together, I feel duty-bound to give it."

Josh watched as Soaring Eagle loaded a visiting mare into the horse trailer that would take her back to her home ranch. Having assumed that Holly was talking to him about the care of Sapphire, the mare she worried over constantly, Soaring Eagle was paying them little attention. "I told you I want to forget that part of my life," Josh stated firmly.

Holly pretended to be inspecting the quality of the hay stored in the barn. "The five years we spent together will never be over, Josh," she said, over her shoulder. "Not entirely. And maybe they shouldn't be, when you consider those years helped make you the man you are today."

Josh caught up with her and pretended to point at something, playing along with the ruse. "I would gladly have done without them."

Holly paused beneath the stairs that led to the upper floor of the loft and looked him up and down in a thoroughly professional way. Her expression was deceptively calm. "Patience McKendrick is getting to you, isn't she?" she guessed grimly.

Hell yes, Patience was getting to him, Josh thought emotionally, and she had been since the first moment he had laid eyes on her again. There wasn't a second that went by that he didn't think about Patience, or wish he could come to her free and clear. But that was impossible. He knew that. He'd reconciled himself to it. So why was he having doubts now? he chided himself sternly.

"You've even started to confide in her," Holly continued.

Josh shrugged, the anger and resentment he'd felt for years spilling over into the present. Legs braced apart, he stood with his arms folded in front of him. "I admit I'd like to tell Patience everything about who I am and why I'm here and why she is dead right not to trust me completely."

For a moment, Holly went very still. For the first time Josh could recall, her face was pale in the risk of danger. "Why haven't you?" she demanded quietly.

Josh sighed, making no effort to hide his regret over how deeply Patience had already been hurt. "Because if I do, I risk Patience's eternal hatred."

"Anything else?"

"I'm afraid if I get too much closer to her that she'll realize why it is I sometimes seem so familiar. I'm afraid she'll realize we have met before, if all too briefly."

Holly's expression became tough as nails, just as Josh expected it would. "You know your whole future is staked to remaining incognito here," she warned.

Josh grimaced. Reaching into his jeans pocket, he pulled out a pocketknife. Flicking open the blade, he cut the twine on a bale of hay and handed Holly a handful of the fresh, fragrant hay. "You don't have to tell me what danger I could be in if my true identity were revealed."

Holly pretended to examine the hay carefully, even going so far as to lift it to her face. "I knew you never should have risked going to the McKendricks for a job. It was too dangerous." She handed the hay back to him.

Josh closed his knife and slipped it back into the pocket of his jeans. "What choice did I have?" he countered, no longer afraid to admit what was, and always had been, in his heart. "You better than anyone know how much I still want it all. Patience is my best, my only hope for ever achieving that."

"You *still* need to be careful," Holly insisted. She regarded him silently. "If I thought there was even a prayer I could change your mind about this—"

"You can't," Josh interrupted stalwartly. Despite his anger with Patience for her lack of trust in him, he was not giving up on them yet.

Holly had known him well enough and long enough to realize when a battle was lost. She smiled at Josh and shrugged in defeat. ''Then there's nothing for me to do except tell you I'll be close enough to help out if you need me,'' she said reluctantly.

Josh nodded. He was hoping that wouldn't be the case. He had his hands full just dealing with his bride-to-be, never mind bringing in Holly—whom Patience was already jealous and suspicious of, too.

''Thanks,'' Josh said tersely.

Holly nodded, repeated her request he call her if he needed her, then left as swiftly and silently as she had come.

As Josh watched her go, he heard a sound in the loft above him. His relief to be rid of Holly was short-lived as he headed for the ladder and was stunned to see Patience on her hands and knees.

He swore softly as their eyes met and held. There was no need for her to say anything. She had clearly heard every word he had said to Holly and was now thinking the worst.

Chapter Eight

Dear Patience,
Should I sleep with a man who is something of a
mystery to me? I love him and he says he is equally
enamored of me, but I am unsure.

Sincerely,
Tempted in Tulsa

Dear Tempted in Tulsa,
Always hold out for all the answers, especially
when in doubt. Only a fool would do otherwise.

You Won't Be Sorry You Waited,
Patience

Feeling he was on the verge of losing everything, Josh
continued up the stairs to the loft. "I see you found
Tweedles and her kittens," he said casually, not sure
exactly how much she had overheard.

"All of them," Patience admitted, casting a glance
at the blissful mother and the six tiny Persian kittens,
who were nursing contentedly.

"We should probably take them back to the house,"
Josh said. Where they could situate the cat and her kit-

tens comfortably and then discuss his conversation with Holly Diehl in private, if need be.

"I agree that would be wise," Patience concurred with a brisk smile, which to his increasing discouragement gave nothing away. She sat back on her heels and regarded him pleasantly. "If you'll just go get a box or something to transport Tweedles and her brood in, we can get to it immediately."

"No problem," Josh said with a great deal more confidence than he felt. He met her gaze with a level one of his own. "Why don't you come with me?"

Patience shook her head and stayed protectively close to her pet. All things considered, her mood was mysteriously calm, Josh thought. "I think I'll stay here and keep an eye on Tweedles," she said. "I think she might take off and hide them again if she figures out what we have planned. New mothers tend to want their privacy."

As did grooms-to-be who were on the run, Josh thought.

"I'll be right back." Knowing there was no time to waste in straightening out this misunderstanding and very much aware they couldn't do it there, where just anyone could come by and overhear, he hurried out of the barn and over to his office. Five minutes later he was back in the hay barn with everything they needed. To his dismay, Tweedles was no longer there. Nor was Patience or the new kittens.

Josh frowned, realizing Patience was getting every bit as good at pulling the wool over his eyes as he was at misdirecting her concerns. Only he had a better reason. A hell of a better reason, he thought as his insides twisted together like a pretzel knot.

His lips pressed together grimly, he headed across the yard to the studio. He was not surprised to find that the door was locked. He dug out his key, then found the door had also been secured with a safety chain. It didn't take a genius to know the other doors were probably similarly secured.

Knowing time was of the essence if he didn't want to lose Patience altogether, he glanced around behind him. Seeing no one in sight, he put his shoulder to the door and rammed his way in, breaking the chain in the process.

Goldie greeted him with a cheerful bark while Josh swept into the house. As he suspected, Patience was in the utility room off the kitchen, seeing to the comfort of Tweedles and her tiny kittens, who were now curled up in a blanket in a corner. Dishes of milk and cat food had been set out. The litter box for Tweedles was situated nearby.

Seeing Josh, Patience stood, stepped out of the utility room and quietly closed the door behind her. "I would've helped you move them," Josh told her.

"Thanks, but I can manage quite fine on my own." Patience walked briskly past. Ignoring Goldie, who was watching them with a mournful face, Patience marched militantly for the back door. She looked like a woman on a mission.

"Now where are you going?" Josh followed reluctantly, unsure which tack to take. He just knew he couldn't let things end here and now. Not this way. Not when he and Patience both were so close to having everything they had ever wanted.

Patience unlatched the chain on the back door, undid the lock with a snap and stepped outside. Her face pale, she announced through her teeth, "I'm going to find Holly Diehl and throw her off Silver Spur property.''

22:36

SENSING IT WOULD do no good at this point to remind Patience that Holly had a contract with the Silver Spur Ranch horse-breeding operation that guaranteed her unlimited access to her pregnant mare, Josh took the only path he could as he joined her outside. ''Mind if I come along?'' To smooth things over and keep the situation from exploding.

Patience tossed her mane of wheat gold hair and sent him a withering look. ''Suit yourself.''

''Thanks,'' he said. ''I will.''

''Which guest room is she in?'' she asked him between tightly gritted teeth as they crossed the yard, side by side.

''Number five.''

Patience stopped dead in her tracks and stared at him with a hauteur that would have turned a lesser man to ice. He knew then she would stop at nothing to make him pay for what she thought he had done to her. ''Which just happens to be adjacent to the ranch manager's cabin, where Max was letting you stay.''

His temper erupted, hot and quick. ''Convenient, wasn't it?'' he drawled sarcastically, letting her know with a look that absolutely nothing had happened.

But she wasn't buying it. ''Don't push me, Josh.''

''Don't push me,'' he warned right back, and enjoyed the trepidation in her eyes just a little bit.

Patience reached Holly's cabin and rapped sharply on her door. No answer. ''Looking for Ms. Diehl?'' Slim asked, passing by.

Patience turned, an artificially bright smile plastered on her face. "Yes. Have you seen her?"

"Went into town again a while ago. Said she'd be back for supper." Slim paused and looked at Patience helpfully. "Anything I can do for you?"

"No." Patience gave him an even more dazzling smile, her eyes glowing with sincere appreciation. "Thanks, Slim."

Slim moved off.

Josh breathed a lengthy sigh of relief. "Thanks for not dragging him into this."

Patience's eyes were hard and accusing as she turned back to Josh. "I wasn't protecting you. I was protecting him."

"I know." Josh paused, aware that the area around the stables was rife with activity this time of day. What they needed was privacy. He wasn't sure he could manage a save at this point, considering all that had just happened, but he knew he needed to try. "Let's go over to my cabin," he coaxed persuasively. "Talk this out. If you don't like what I have to say, then you can kick me off the property. But at least hear me out, Patience. If nothing else, it'll give you a chance to satisfy your curiosity," he finished gently, making what he hoped was an offer she couldn't refuse.

He could see the journalist in her needed answers as much as the woman. "Five minutes," Patience decreed finally.

Josh nodded. "Fair enough."

They crossed the yard to his quarters in stony silence. Arms folded defiantly in front of her, Patience waited for him to open the door. Dropping her fists to her sides, she followed him inside.

IT WAS THE FIRST TIME Patience had been inside the sparsely furnished manager's cabin since Josh had been there. Knowing he had been living there for several months, she was stunned to see how little he had done to make it a home. Oh, there was a stack of veterinary medicine journals beside the single reading chair, a laptop computer on the desk, a small, thirteen-inch color television. And it was almost obsessively neat. There were no dishes in the stainless steel sink. Nothing on the small electric stove or the pineboard counters. The double bed in the small adjacent bedroom was neatly made with a navy-blue-and-pine-green plaid quilt. There was no sign of a woman anywhere, no sign Holly had even been inside. It was strictly, Patience thought, a man's domain. A loner's domain.

Josh strode to the refrigerator. He pulled out a jug of apple cider and poured them each a glass. Their fingers brushed as he handed it to her. "You saw me with Holly, didn't you?"

Determined to keep her head, Patience sipped at the cool, sweet liquid. Forcing herself to relax a bit, she held Josh's eyes as the cider moistened her parched throat. "You know I did."

Josh downed his own cider in a single gulp, then poured himself another tall glass. "How much did you overhear?" he demanded.

Patience tossed her head, sending her hair flying in a silken whirl around her face. "Enough to know my Uncle Max had you pegged all wrong!"

Abruptly, his eyes turned bleak. "It wasn't what it seemed," he said flatly.

Patience widened her eyes at him in a deliberately taunting manner. "Oh, really?" she prompted, baiting him even more boldly in an effort to make him lose his temper, too, so they could finally get at the whole truth. She set her half-full glass down with an unhappy thud on the small kitchen table. "Then perhaps you would like to start by explaining Holly's concern for you." She trod closer. "Not to mention the intimate past you two seem to have. Tell me, Josh," she demanded jealously as her rioting emotions took over once again, "is Holly the woman you told me about earlier, the one you loved and lost?"

"No," Josh said. To Patience's irritation, his gray eyes were completely free of remorse. "That was someone else," he continued affably. "Holly and I were just friends. We lived in the same town house complex and got to know each other while I was in college and veterinary school, but we were not—and I stress *not*—romantically involved."

"But you were close," Patience said as she speared him with a censuring gaze, hurt he had deliberately kept her in the dark about the full nature of his relationship with Holly. If it was all so innocent, as he kept asserting, why hadn't he told her all this from the very beginning, when he introduced them?

"And she knows things about you. Intimate things."

Josh's jaw set as he regarded her with a mixture of exasperation and annoyance. "She was a confidante, years ago, at a time when I had a lot on my mind and needed a friend. These days, except for when she initiates a meeting or conversation, or comes to visit the horse she has stabled here, I rarely see her, and frankly I like it that way." His mouth thinned. "Holly's a nice woman, a good woman, but she can also be a real pain in the butt because she tends to meddle too damn much! As you may have gathered," he concluded grimly, "I don't like people prying into my personal life."

Patience was silent a moment. From what she had seen thus far, Josh's behavior toward Holly bore out everything he had said. She hadn't seen them kissing or looking starry-eyed at each other. Their conversation was damning and intimate, true, but as Patience thought about the intimacy of her relationship with Cisco, she knew that that, too, could be easily misinterpreted. And already had been by Josh, at least a little. But she and Cisco were, and always had been, just friends.

Yet despite all that, Patience knew there were some things she had overheard Holly and Josh saying that had to be explained. And she wasn't going to rest until they were. She regarded Josh grimly. "Why did you tell Holly that I'm dead right not to trust you completely, or that you want to hide the reason why you seem so familiar to me? And why does Holly consider it essential you remain here only if you do so incognito?"

"I know it all sounds bad." Josh watched her roam the small living area.

"Not just sounds bad, Josh." Patience skidded to a halt in front of him and suppressed the urge to deck him. "It is bad. You have been using me and perhaps the McKendrick fortune to help you 'get it all,' whatever that is."

He stared at her in frustration, but there was no masking the potent yearning in his face. "That, Patience, is happiness. A life, family, a woman to love. That's what I was talking about when I said I was so close to having everything I had ever wanted."

Patience desperately wanted to believe that. If she looked into his eyes much longer, she knew she would. "Tell me, Josh, is Holly Diehl going to be hurt by whatever scheme you have going here? Or is she going to gain, too, and it's just me that stands to lose in all this?'' The way she had lost before, with Alec.

"You won't lose anything by your association with me, Patience," Josh said quietly, putting both his hands on her shoulders. "I give you my word on that."

Patience shoved the heel of her hand through the mussed layers of her hair and emitted a short, bitter laugh. "Don't you understand? I already have lost, just by trusting you for a little while."

He shook his head. "You misunderstood," he repeated flatly.

Had she? Thus far, he really hadn't explained much of anything. Patience smiled at him sarcastically and knew that he was still hiding every bit as much as he was revealing to her. "I don't think so," she replied in a soft, bitter voice, furious she had been made a fool of once again. "You see, Josh, I know when I have been lied to," she said softly, tears stinging her eyes. "And you have lied to me from the very start of this ridiculous 'engagement' of ours. And probably Max, as well."

He tightened his hold on her possessively. "Listen to me, Patience. Nothing is what it seems."

"Tell you what." Patience flung herself away from him. "We'll let Cisco and my brothers sort it all out. Maybe they can figure out who you really are and why I am dead right not to trust you. Maybe they can help me figure out just where it was that you and I have met before, and why you don't want me to recall any of it."

For a second, a flicker of hurt was reflected in his silver-gray eyes. It was gone as quickly as it appeared, making Patience wonder if she had really seen it there at all. Or had she just wanted to see it? "Give me a chance to explain," he urged gruffly.

"Why should I?" Patience retorted fiercely, the hurt inside her mounting to an unmanageable level. "When all you've done is make a fool out of me and Max and heaven only knows who else from the very first!" She stepped past him militantly.

He crossed his arms over his chest, his actions as slow and deliberate as hers had been impulsive. "Where are you going?"

Patience shrugged and refused to turn around to look at him. "It doesn't matter," she stated defiantly, knowing it was true, "as long as I am far away from you."

Josh moved between her and the door. "I'm sorry, Patience." He regarded her implacably, every inch of him tensed and ready for battle. "I'm afraid I can't let you do that."

"GET OUT OF MY WAY, JOSH."

So it had come to this, Josh thought as he met Patience's dagger-eyed stare equably. "Not until we find a way to work this out," he said with quiet authority. He did not want to get in a wrestling match with her. He preferred to talk this out calmly and quietly, but if she gave him no choice, he would do what was required, just as he had done what was required of him years ago. And the sooner she understood that, the better.

Patience picked up the gauntlet. "First you tell me where exactly we have met before."

He regarded her in stony silence, knowing he couldn't answer. Patience's frustration mounted, as he had expected it would.

"Your showing up here on the ranch was no accident, was it?"

He felt the fury swirling around them. "No. It wasn't," he said wearily.

Patience reeled backward, as if he had slapped her. "Then why are you here?" she demanded emotionally, looking as if she might burst into tears at any second.

It was all Josh could do not to drag her into his arms and kiss her and hold her until the pain in her eyes went away. "Because I know what Alec put you through," he said hoarsely, wishing like hell he could tell her everything, "and I wanted to see if you were all right."

She blinked. "And yet you expected me to hate you if I ever found any of this out."

Josh edged toward her, aware his bleak prophecy was already coming true despite all the pains he had taken to try to protect her from just this. "I've already told you all I can, Patience," he said sternly. "You're just going to have to trust me."

"How can I do that when I just heard you and Holly Diehl admit the five years the two of you spent together won't ever really be over!" The tears she had been holding back poured down her cheeks.

"Nothing of our past ever will be, Patience," Josh told her with strained equanimity as he advanced on her slowly, deliberately. "Our past is what makes us who we are today."

Patience couldn't dispute the truth of that. "And yet you, Josh, want me to forget all about Alec!" she cried, even more upset.

"Because he was the wrong man for you," Josh said flatly. Because he never would have been strong enough to protect you.

"I will never believe that," Patience swore, whirling away from Josh once again. She returned to her half-finished glass of cider and picked it up with shaking hands.

His heart going out to her, Josh watched her gulp it down. "I didn't say he meant to hurt you," he told her softly.

Patience wiped the tears away with the back of her hand. "Then why did he leave me the way he did?"

He could see the fight draining out of her as swiftly as it had appeared. The situation was still bad, he reassured himself firmly, but not unsalvageable, and it wouldn't be unless he lost his head. "That I can't tell you."

Patience swung around to face him. "And I am supposed to just accept that and not ask anything else," she retorted, her lower lip trembling.

"Yes." He stepped close and took her in his arms.

"Damn it, Josh—" she wedged her forearms between them "—you have to know I can't leave it at that."

"If you don't, Patience, you are going to end up putting us both in danger."

Her blue eyes blazed. Without warning, the truth of all he had told her was beginning to sink in, and he could see she was beginning to believe him. "How?" she whispered, her hands flattening across his chest.

If only he could tell her everything, but that was out of the question and always had been. Josh tightened his hold on her and released an exasperated breath. "You're better off not knowing." If only he could make her believe that.

She stiffened and gave him a withering glance. "I was better off never having met you!"

Josh sighed. "As much as I hate to admit it, I agree."

Abruptly, she stared up at him. "Tell me how I know you," she whispered emotionally. "Tell me why you seem so familiar."

Josh gritted his teeth. The last thing he wanted was her remembering anything, especially now. The emotions they were both feeling were dangerous. That was why he had avoided them these many years. But they also made him feel alive. They made him feel like taking risks. "You're just going to have to forget you ever heard that," he said gruffly, still wanting to protect her, if necessary with his life.

A combination of melancholy and hurt filled her eyes. Abruptly, she seemed on the verge of tears again. "You're asking too much," she murmured.

The way she looked at him, he could tell she wanted to believe him. She wanted to believe in him with all her heart and soul. It was up to him to make that happen. "The way things look to you right now, I know you don't have any reason to trust me. But everything I have done, I have done to protect you," Josh told her gently as he smoothed the hair from her face. "If I could have made it so that Alec could have come back to you, I would have," he confided emotionally, telling her all that was in his heart and had been for many years. "But it didn't work out that way." He ran one hand down her spine, cupped the other beneath her chin.

Her blue eyes widened as she struggled to understand. "So instead you decided to come here and take his place, is that it? *You're* here in his stead?"

Josh tried not to think about how good she felt as he held her in his arms again, how right, and how much he wanted to make love to her again and again and again. "It's what you wanted, isn't it?" he murmured as his hands skimmed up her sides, over her ribs. "Alec back?

And if not him, the next best thing, someone who knew him intimately, someone who knew how much he loved and desired and cherished you." He drew the pad of his thumb across her lower lip, reveling in the softness. "Someone who knew how to kiss you." He traced the bow-shaped curve of her upper lip and watched her eyes grow smoky with passion. "Someone who knew how much you needed to be loved, held, touched." And she did need that, he thought. So did he.

"Josh—"

His touch as gentle as he could make it, he gathered her close again and worked his hands down her spine. "Tell me you don't want me," he whispered. Hands on her hips, he tugged her close, fitted her intimately against him.

Patience closed her eyes and rested her forehead against his. The warmth of her breath brushed his cheek. Her breathing was every bit as unsteady as his, her body soft and giving as she confessed, "You know I can't."

He kissed her brow, the shell of her ear, the slope of her throat, and gloried in her soft, trembling response, even as he was impatient for more. "Tell me you haven't been lonely," he urged.

Her hands curled around his shoulders, held tight. She moaned soft and low as he found her lips again. And then her throat. "I can't."

Knowing the bedroom was where they both wanted to be, Josh picked Patience up in his arms and carried her there. He set her down on the covers and lay beside her.

Pleased she hadn't uttered a sound of protest, he rolled so she was beneath him, the softness of her length fitted closely against the hardness of his.

Threading his hands through the silk of her hair, he urged softly, ''Tell me you haven't wished that every day and every night since Alec left you could have this kind of closeness and intimacy in your life again, that you could feel so close to someone it was almost as if you were two halves of a whole.'' He knew it was all he had dreamed about. Wanted. Despaired over. For what seemed forever. And try as he might, he couldn't just walk away from her. Not again, even if, damn it all, she *didn't* remember this... and she should.

''You think you can do this for me... make me forget? Make me want to go on?'' She sucked in a tremulous breath as he bent and kissed her, and Josh knew from the way she responded to him that his just being there had opened up possibilities for her that had not existed before.

''I know,'' he promised, kissing her deeply. He sifted her hair through his hands and fitted his lips to hers for another long, leisurely kiss. He held her tight, knowing that despite the irony of it all, there was no better man for the task. No one who would love her more.

Then, looking her straight in the eye he passionately repeated, ''I know.'' And no matter what happened after this, today he knew he would remember this moment for the rest of his life.

Patience knew she should fight him. After everything she had seen and overheard, she had no reason to trust Josh. But she did. She had no reason to want him in her life and in her bed. But she did.

Listen to your hearts. 'Cause if you do, I guarantee you'll know what to do, Max had said in his last message to her. And her heart was telling her that Josh was not what his furtive conversation with Holly Diehl would have her believe. Her heart told her that Josh was the kind of man who would always be on the right side of the law.

He was the man who had taken charge of the horse operation for Max, the man who had teased and provoked and held her tight. He was the man who had kissed her with shattering intensity, catapulting her from her outwardly successful but lonely existence into the tumultuous yet satisfying present.

Max wouldn't have trusted Josh if he hadn't believed he was good for me, Patience reassured herself firmly. Max wouldn't have suggested we have a child together. Max wouldn't have left part of the ranch to Josh unless he had thoroughly checked Josh out, if he hadn't believed Josh was on the right side of the law, too. Was it possible, Patience wondered, shocked, that Josh was here incognito on some sort of official government business? If so, that would certainly explain Holly's demand he remain here only if he could do so incognito.

"Let go of the past, Patience, and just believe in us," Josh whispered between long, drugging kisses. His hands swept over her, lovingly charting her dips and curves, the tenderness in his touch freeing them from everything but the moment and each other.

How long had it been since she had really taken a chance on anything, never mind the kind of reckless yet satisfying love he was promising? Here was her chance, Patience thought, awash in pleasure, to make her dream of having a baby a reality....

And suddenly she knew she could no more resist the chance to discover what lay at the very heart of this whirlpool of danger and excitement she found herself in than she could dive back into the self-imposed co-

coon of celibacy in which she'd been hiding these last seventeen years.

As his lips touched hers, she cried out softly and surged against him, the passion between them so strong and so right and so total it didn't seem quite real. His hands were moving over her, unfastening the buttons on her blouse, parting the edges to reveal the lace-edged cotton camisole beneath. He tugged it from the waistband of her jeans and slid his hand beneath it, his nimble fingers ghosting over the curves of her breasts and settling warmly on the jutting crowns. A deep heat began in her middle, radiating outward in searing waves, and suddenly it became important to be touching everywhere.

Still kissing, she reached for the buttons on his shirt. He reached for the zipper on her jeans. Efficient moments later, their clothes landed in a heap on the floor. And then they were kissing again, losing themselves on that glorious edge between heaven and hell. His fingers were searching out the silken core of her, and she was lifting her hips, pleading wordlessly for a more intimate union.

Josh wanted to prolong Patience's pleasure, bring her to the brink again and again and again, but she was beyond waiting as she cradled him in her hands and urged him close, first to the sensitive entrance to her being, then just inside. Holding back with all his might, Josh reached for the foil packet in his jeans. He had never reacted to a woman's touch with such all-consuming need, but there were precautions to take before this went any further.

She caught his hips in her hands, moving against him in imperative circles that drove him ever closer to the edge. "No. Now, Josh," she breathed restlessly in a way that told him that nothing was more important than holding on to the hope of love and the promise of the future. As he looked into her eyes, he saw she trusted him completely. She trusted him with her heart. It meant the world to him.

"I want this," she whispered, her expression as stubbornly insistent as it was hopelessly romantic. And he knew then, even if she hadn't yet dared to say the words to him, that she was falling in love with him, too. "I want your child," she whispered softly. "I want you."

Maybe they had both played it safe for too long, Josh thought. Maybe it was time he took a chance, not only on the present and Patience, but on their future together, as well. "I want you, too, sweetheart." *I want to preserve this moment for eternity.* "I want our baby."

Slipping a pillow beneath her hips, he lifted her up and eased into her, being careful not to overwhelm her with his size and weight. And then they were kissing again, the soul-searing sensuality of their coupling shaking them to the core, calling forth a response that dazed and drove them both. He kissed her and held her, touched and took her, until they were both drunk on the sensations of overheated bodies and clinging lips, until his need for her was like a thick, aching pain inside of him that would not, could not be eased. Until they were nearly one, heart and soul.

"Damn, Patience—" His self-control evaporated, as did hers. When she locked herself around him, he drove deep, glorying in the trembling sensations, deliberately intensifying the breathless pleasure. And then they were spinning out of control, into the rich seduction of oblivion.

PATIENCE LAY wrapped in Josh's arms, every inch of her deliciously sated and trembling, one thought rushing through her mind over and over again. *We just made a baby.*

Intellectually, of course, she knew it was too soon to tell. But she felt the distinct possibility of new life in her heart and in her soul. And she knew if she hadn't succeeded in creating a child with Josh this evening, she was most definitely willing to try again and again and again.

The old-fashioned way. Just as Josh—and even Uncle Max—had wanted.

Smiling, she extricated herself enough to rise up on one elbow. And that was when she noticed what she had failed to see before. "What is this?" She touched the scars on his shoulder. The ones on his knee. The jagged one running down his chest, just beneath his ribs. "What happened?"

Josh shook his head, as if he didn't want to spoil the miracle of their passionate lovemaking by talking about that. He caught her hand and pressed a kiss to her fingertips. "It was a long time ago."

But it had still happened, Patience thought, upset. Her throat ached. "I can't bear the thought of you in pain." And if he was some kind of undercover law officer, as she half suspected, then his life would be in danger.

His expression unperturbed, he drew her close. "Then don't."

"Josh—"

Rolling so she was beneath him once again, he kissed her breathless until she melted against him once again. Yet even as he swept his hands down her body, evoking a passionate response from them both, Patience knew that making love again would not solve all their problems, even if it was the only solution he had to offer them. Finally, he drew back, looking down into her still-troubled eyes as if to gauge her skyrocketing emotions. "You're never going to tell me everything, are you?" she whispered.

He grimaced, letting her know in an instant he was not about to make his struggles hers. "Forget the past, Patience," he advised her softly, gathering her close. "Enjoy the present."

But how could she? Patience wondered as he quickly shut her out of his life again. What secrets was Josh still holding from her? Reality came crashing down on her, and she realized just exactly what it was she had done, the risks she had just taken, the kind of risk she would warn her readers never ever to take. It was time for some cool thinking. She couldn't do that as long as they were both holding each other this way.

Grabbing her clothes, she began to get dressed.

He sighed. Looked disappointed, but not surprised. "You're angry again, aren't you?"

Angry? Hurt? What was the difference, when he had just shut her out again, big-time? She threw her clothes on haphazardly while he reluctantly did the same. "Who are you, Josh? Who are you really?" Patience demanded as she snatched up her jeans. And how was it possible that he, a relative stranger to her, could so quickly and effectively reach her heart in a way no one save Alec Vaughn, long ago, had ever done?

He watched her tug on her jeans while he slipped on his own. "I'm exactly who you think." He shrugged on his shirt. His eyes on hers, he buttoned the edges together calmly. "Dr. Josh Colter."

Patience put on her blouse, realized too late she had buttoned it up crookedly and had to start all over again.

He followed her around the room, while more and more she felt like a fool. "Just say it, Patience," he ordered gruffly while she sat down on the edge of the bed to yank on her boots.

She let her booted feet hit the floor with a disgruntled thud. Hands braced on either side of her, she stayed where she was and tipped her head to his. "All right, I will. What else do you know about Alec's disappearance from my life? What haven't you told me?" If Josh was a law officer, he had to know something, especially if Alec's life and Josh's had been somehow intertwined.

Josh leaned against the bureau, his expression becoming both brooding and frustratingly distant once again. "I couldn't have prevented Alec from jilting you, if that's what you're asking," he replied. "By the time I had more or less stumbled onto...things...just as you have, and witnessed some things I shouldn't have seen, crucial decisions had already been made and Alec's fate was sealed." He paused, his broad shoulders tensing beneath the soft cotton fabric of his shirt. He regarded her, an uncompromising glint in his gray eyes. "The bottom line is that Alec Vaughn inadvertently got involved with some very bad people around the time of your wedding. The way things were then, he had no choice. He had to disappear for a while. He couldn't come back to you, because then he would've been putting you in danger. And I know for a fact that he wanted you to be safe more than anything, because he did love you, Patience, with all his heart."

Patience took solace in that much. So she hadn't been wrong about the genuineness of Alec's feelings for her after all.

"Five years after all of that, he died," Josh continued.

"You're telling me his death was not an accident?"

Josh's eyes were haunted as he grimaced and speared her with a level look. "The newspapers said it was pneumonia and I accept that, as I recommend you do. If you want to be safe, if you want the baby we may just have made to be safe, you will not ask me any more questions, period."

They stared at each other in silence.

Patience had only to look into Josh's eyes to know he was keeping his own confidence as a way of protecting her, too, and that there would or could be no negotiating with him on this subject.

The strange thing was, she really wanted to trust Josh. Whether she liked it or not, the danger in pushing too hard for the truth from him was very real; if she went too far, she sensed he would simply walk away and she would never see him again. And yet, by the same token, how could she have a future with Josh without knowing everything there was to know about him? Wasn't there danger in that, too?

Just then, the phone began to ring. Josh went to answer it. He listened intently, then said, "I'll be right there," and hung up. As he turned back to Patience, his expression was unaccountably grim.

"What is it?" Patience asked, alarmed.

"It's Mandy," Josh replied. "She's started to have her foal and she's in trouble."

Chapter Nine

Dear Patience,
I see my long-lost love in someone else. Is it possible he was reincarnated?

Sincerely,
Still in the Past

Dear Still in the Past,
Get glasses. You're imagining things.
Don't Be Caught Singing off the Wrong Song Sheet,

Patience

"How did Mandy get in the second stage of labor without anyone noticing she was foaling?" Patience asked as she and Josh left his quarters and headed quickly over toward the foaling barn.

"Sometimes a mare can slip through the first stage of labor without having any contractions you can see, and move right into the second phase, which seems to be what is happening with Mandy."

"You're worried."

"According to Soaring Eagle, Mandy's water broke a few minutes ago. There's no sign of the outer sac yet."

Patience struggled to recall what she knew. "And that should have occurred right away, with the onrush of the water, right?"

Josh nodded. "Normally, you'd be able to see one foot, which is why Soaring Eagle telephoned."

Soaring Eagle was inside the foaling stall, talking soothingly to Mandy and carefully washing her hindquarters and perineal area in preparation for the delivery of the foal.

Mandy was lying down on her side, her chestnut coat slippery with sweat. Her tail had been bandaged from the end to just below the bone of the tail to keep it out of the way during the birth. As Josh entered the stall, she rose up on her sternum, then lumbered slowly and clumsily to her feet.

"She's been up and down several times," Soaring Eagle said, handing Josh his medical kit. "Can't seem to get comfortable."

Patience watched as Mandy suffered another contraction and another, her pendulous abdomen tensing visibly with the strain. Without warning, she dropped down again and lay back so all four legs were extended stiffly away from her body. She was lathered in sweat. After another thirty-second interval, she suffered another contraction.

And another. "She really seems to be in tremendous pain," Patience worried.

"I know." Josh tugged on a pair of surgical gloves and knelt down beside Mandy and examined her briefly. "The foal must be stuck."

Slim strode in breathlessly, sweat streaming from beneath the brim of his hat. He looked stressed to the max as he announced to one and all, "That colt that's not halterbroke is going wild. Refuses to come in from the pasture and he's already kicked one of the handlers. If Josh and Patience can spare you, Soaring Eagle, maybe you could see if you could calm him?"

"Go on, both of you," Josh said, his glance and manner steady. "Patience and I will handle things here."

The two men slipped off. Josh and Patience were alone with the struggling mare. "Slip on a pair of gloves," Josh directed calmly, apparently having no qualms about her ability to help him with the impending birth. "I need you to give me a hand with the foal."

Patience knelt beside him and Mandy. Anxiously, she noted that the edge of the gray outer sac surrounding the foal was visible, but there was still no evidence of the colt's foot. Josh didn't have to tell her that was a bad sign.

Josh reached inside Mandy and carefully ruptured the sac that had protected the foal during parturition. Working gently but quickly, he dislodged the foot. Patience breathed a sigh of relief as he eased it out of the birth canal. Within minutes the second forefoot was visible, then the foal's muzzle.

While Patience soothed the mare with a gentle voice and soft strokes of her palm, Mandy continued to labor hard, her sides heaving with the force of every contraction, her entire body lathered in sweat, until at last the foal's head and neck appeared. Again, she paused, breathing hard and trembling from head to foot.

"Why is she stopping?" Patience asked, as Josh carefully peeled the outer sac from the foal's face and checked to make sure the cord was still intact and not wrapped around the foal's neck.

"She's exhausted," Josh replied. "Probably needs a minute to collect herself." One hand still on the emerging foal, he patted Mandy's flank reassuringly. "C'mon, girl, don't give up on me now," Josh urged quietly. "Not much more. We need to get this baby out of there."

Whether she understood what Josh was saying or was just ready to try again, Mandy worked to expel her foal. Two more contractions and the foal's head and neck appeared. Then one shoulder, spindly brown chest, abdomen, hips and hind legs. Both arms extended, Patience helped catch the still, lifeless foal.

"She's not breathing," Patience said, beginning to panic despite herself.

"I know." Josh grabbed the bulb syringe out of his medical kit and cleared the foal's nasal passages. "Nothing. Looks like we're going to have to apply oxygen." He slipped a mask on the foal.

Patience waited and prayed his efforts to resuscitate the beautiful chestnut foal would be successful.

Finally, the foal shuddered, opened her eyes and seemed to be breathing on her own, while her exhausted mama went into a comfortable resting state.

Elated that all was well, Josh and Patience exchanged tremulous grins. "We did it!" Patience said, tears of happiness shimmering in her eyes.

"We sure did," Josh said. With Patience's help, he began to pull off the rest of the amniotic sac. When that was done, Patience took one of the towels Soaring Eagle had brought into the stall earlier and began the process of vigorously toweling the soaked, shaking foal dry, working at the same time to stimulate warmth, respiration and circulation.

"You look like you've done this before," Josh remarked approvingly to Patience, watching as she took great care not to disturb the still-pulsing umbilical cord.

She nodded. "It was the only part of the birth Uncle Max would ever let me assist in," Patience said.

When she had finished, she and Josh curled the foal close to Mandy's hindquarters and held her there as they waited for the oxygenated and enriched blood to pass from Mandy to her new foal.

Satisfied the foal was now successfully breathing on her own, Josh first reduced, then removed the oxygen and clear plastic mask from the foal's face. Working in unison, he and Patience waited another minute, then, seeing the umbilical cord was no longer pulsing, let go of the sleek foal. She kicked away from her mama with instinctive force, severing the umbilical cord in the process. Josh quickly applied navel antiseptic to protect against infection.

Josh and Patience waited to see what Mandy was going to do. When she did not rise to her feet, they scooted the foal around to her head. Oblivious to the others in the stall, Mandy inspected her newborn, then began to lick her clean. The foal, looking as if she were in seventh heaven to be attended so tenderly, cuddled even closer to her mama.

Patience felt her eyes fill with tears of happiness. She looked over at Josh, who seemed inordinately happy and relieved at the joyous outcome, too. If this was what it was like to share the birth of a foal, what would it be like to share the birth of their child? she wondered. And knew more than anything she wanted to find out.

"Pretty neat, huh?" Josh said happily.

"As many times as I've seen a mare give birth, it never loses its miracle quality for me," she told Josh softly, wondering if there was anything more satisfying than bringing new life into the world. And she knew it must be even more incredible to bring your own child into this world, especially knowing your child was the result of a great and wonderful love.

"That's because it is a miracle," Josh said as he quickly and expertly cleansed and prepared the udder for nursing.

As if on cue, the foal struggled to her feet on spindly legs. Mandy followed. At first, the foal was unable to find the proper location to nurse, so Josh and Patience guided her gently to the appropriate spot on her mama's belly. She took in only six swallows of colostrum before she fell back, content but exhausted, into the straw.

While her newborn rested, Mandy went into the last part of labor, expelling the placenta that had nourished her foal in the womb. Josh made sure everything was as it should be, then stitched Mandy up while Patience soothed the mare and attended her foal.

When he was through with Mandy, Josh gave the foal tetanus and Penstrep injections. "So what are you going to call her?" Patience asked.

Josh thought about it a minute. "How about Impatience?" he teased. "Since she was in such a hurry to be born."

"Get serious."

"I am. An extraordinary filly should have an extraordinary name, don't you think?"

Patience thought about the chestnut colt they had just delivered, with the long, streaked white nose and dark black forelock and mane. She released a soft, contented sigh. "She is beautiful."

Josh leaned toward her and tucked a strand of hair behind her ear. "So are you. And our babies will be, too. And I do intend to have some with you, Patience." He bent toward her, their lips met, and they kissed with a tenderness that went all the way to her soul.

Slowly, they drew apart, and Patience knew the magic Max had wanted for them was descending on them full force.

"IF IT WEREN'T for the terms of Max's will, I'd tell you to go on back to the house," Josh said after a moment. The truth was, he wanted to make love to her desperately, but he couldn't leave until Soaring Eagle came back to take over the postpartum care of the mare and her foal.

"No problem," Patience said softly. To Josh's relief, she seemed as eager to be with him as he was to be with her. "I don't mind waiting," she confided as she scooted even closer to Josh. "Besides, I want to be here to take care of Mandy and Impatience."

Seeing what a natural Patience was around the stables, Josh understood why Max had wanted to give the horse operation to her. She would love it just as Max had. "Did you hang out here much when you were growing up?" he asked.

Patience nodded and drew her knees up to her chest. "As much as I could. I was pretty busy with school and family activities."

Josh could imagine that she had been. From what he saw, Patience never seemed to sit still for a moment. "Did you get attached to any of the foals?" he asked casually, knowing that no matter what happened in the future, he would remember this moment in time, and the way they'd made love earlier, forever.

"Only once," Patience admitted softly. "I fell in love with a foal that had already been promised to a buyer." She shook her head regretfully, remembering, and turned her eyes to his. "Max warned me not to get so emotionally involved with the animal, but I was there when he was born, and I just couldn't help it. When he went off to the owner's farm after he had been weaned from his mama, it about broke my heart," she admitted in a voice that quavered.

Josh couldn't be sure, but he thought there was a film of tears shimmering in her eyes.

"After that, I was a little more careful. I didn't visit any single foal enough to get my heart broken again."

And she had done the same after Alec, too, Josh thought. Not allowing herself to get involved with any other men. Though he couldn't say he was all that disappointed about that.

"Who does Impatience belong to?" Patience asked.

"Me." Josh brushed his knuckles across her cheek and knew that this was yet another bond between them. "So you can visit her anytime you want," he promised. "I'll make sure of that."

GOLDIE LAY at Patience's feet. Patience reached down to pet the golden retriever on the head. "I know. You want to get out to see your sweetheart again. But you are not the only one having problems, Goldie."

Goldie looked up at her with sober black eyes.

"I have another column to write. It's due by tomorrow evening. The only problem is, I just can't concentrate."

"Maybe you just need something to eat and a good night's sleep," Josh suggested, sticking his head in the studio door.

It was more than just that keeping her mind from her work, Patience thought. It was because of Alec, and all she still didn't know about the circumstances surrounding his death.

Oblivious to her prickly mood, Josh suggested affably, "Why don't I see what I can rustle up for supper?"

Patience nodded. It had been hours since they had eaten lunch and she was hungry, too. "I'll be in to help in a minute," Patience said a little distractedly.

As soon as Josh had disappeared, she turned her computer back on. Going through the newspaper syndicate's data bank, she made an E-mail request for information on mob activity in the Yale area around the time of her wedding and Alec's disappearance, and again in Louisiana around the time of his death, five years later. She also wanted to get a look at the obituary that said he had died of pneumonia. And she wanted to know more about Holly Diehl. Just who was she? And how and why had Josh been involved with Holly? Was it possible the two of them were both federal agents, involved in some kind of ongoing investigation? And if so, why didn't Josh just tell her that? Surely he knew by now he could trust her to keep his confidence.

At the sound of rapid keystrokes, Goldie perked her head up. Patience felt a flash of guilt. She pushed it away. "I have to do this, girl," she told Josh's dog.

Goldie tilted her head slightly to the side.

"I know Josh thinks I would be safer if I remained in the dark about everything that went on back then, and now, but I have to know," Patience whispered. One way or another she was going to find out the whole truth, whether Josh helped her or not. And then, and only then, would she decide if she should further her involvement with Josh, because like it or not, she was precariously close to falling deeply, irrevocably, head-over-heels in love with him.

Patience forwarded the request for information via electronic mail, then switched off her computer. "In the meantime, I guess I better get in there and help Josh in the kitchen."

She headed that way, Goldie trotting happily after her. Since they had returned Wrangler to his owners, he hadn't been back. As a result, Goldie—who was still in heat—was much happier in a general sense, though still seemed to be feeling the effects of unrequited love. Which in turn made Patience wonder if maybe the key to happiness was simply getting rid of the male in your life who was constantly tempting and exciting you and yet making you miserable.... At the moment, Goldie sure seemed better off.

Josh was standing in front of the refrigerator, peering at the contents thoughtfully. "What are you in the mood for? Hot? Cold? Sweet? Spicy?"

Patience shrugged, knowing all she really wanted was answers to all her questions. But that was something she was not likely to get. "Surprise me," she said indifferently.

Without telling her what the end result was going to be, Josh got out a package of bacon, a bowl of fruit, milk, eggs, flour, oil, baking powder and salt. "Just sit and keep me company," he said, waving at a chair. "I'll do everything."

Patience watched him layer bacon strips in a skillet and place it on the stove.

"You're still a little jumpy, restless tonight," he noticed.

Patience looked in the utility room, where Tweedles and her kittens were comfortably ensconced, then out the window above the sink. The wind was whipping up something fierce. The scent of impending rain hung in the air. In the distance, she thought she saw some lightning flash. The coming storm fitted her mood exactly. She turned back to him, feeling more disgruntled than ever with their situation and the fact they were supposed to be married in less than nineteen hours. It hadn't helped that her brother Cody had visited a short while ago and was having problems in the romance department himself.

"I guess I am a little moody," Patience said finally, turning away. She didn't want him to see everything she was thinking and feeling right now. It made her far too vulnerable.

Josh came up behind her and wrapped his arms around her waist. He fitted himself intimately against her and nuzzled the top of her head. "Is it because we might have made a baby this evening?"

Patience bit her lip as thunder rolled in the sky overhead. "I admit I'm a little worried about it." She turned around to face him, wanting him to understand this much. "I've never behaved so recklessly in my life. Except—" She stopped and couldn't go on.

"With Alec?" he said, barely seeming to breathe as he waited for her reply.

Patience flattened her hands on the broad width of his shoulders, aware she had never felt more entranced by a man, or more confused. She wanted to be with

Josh, and she didn't. The bottom line was it really bothered her that he just flat refused to tell her everything about himself. "I don't know what got into me tonight."

His pewter eyes darkened the way they always did when he was about to kiss her. "Passion, maybe?" he said softly.

Patience jerked in a breath and pushed out of the warm circle of his arms. This was all beginning to feel too comfortable to her, and common sense told her it shouldn't. Her pulse pounding, she walked to the far side of the kitchen. Still facing him, she leaned against the counter. "I feel like a fool, writing letters of advice to readers. Telling them to be practical, to be guided by common sense first and then their hearts. Only to find myself embarking on a wild, dangerous love affair with a man I barely know. A man my Uncle Max arranged for me to marry by providing an enormous dowry no man could resist." Spelled out that way, the whole idea was ludicrous. He had to know it, too.

Josh put an arm on either side of her, caging her against the length of him, and leaned in close. "Is that what we're having, Patience, a wild, dangerous love affair?"

Judging from the hot glimmer in his eyes, he liked the sound of that. "Maybe I should have said 'tryst.'"

He brushed his lips down the curve of her neck, starting wildfires wherever he touched. "I think I like 'love affair' better."

Patience closed her eyes, luxuriating in the feelings, even as she knew she couldn't permit them to go on. "Whatever it was, Josh, it can't happen again until we know each other a lot better."

JOSH KNEW HE WAS WALKING a tightrope, that he must not reveal too much about himself. And yet he had to open up enough to let her know that she could trust him intimately in a way she never would have trusted Alec again. "Why not?" he asked her softly.

"Because it would be foolish of us to rush into this any more than we already have, and I'm not foolish," Patience replied in a low, anguished voice. She bit her lower lip. "Because we barely know each other."

And because, he thought, she felt vulnerable when she was with him. Too vulnerable for comfort. "That can be rectified," he persuaded, still hoping they would make love again and again through the coming night.

Patience did not look as sure. "How can it be rectified?" she demanded emotionally.

He shrugged, and only because he knew that to make love to her now would be to lose her, he gently let her go. "I'll tell you whatever it is you want to know, within the parameters we've already set up."

She thought about that a moment. "All right," she said finally, her blue eyes more serious and direct than he had ever seen them, "what was your early life like?"

Josh shrugged. "Kind of like yours, I guess. Rife with turmoil. My mom died when I was nine. My dad was not really into parenting, and as a result, he and I were never very close."

"What did he do?"

Josh broke two eggs into a bowl. "He owned his own business. He had several stores, and he was always going from one location to another, overseeing operations."

"He must have been pretty successful, then."

Josh frowned as he measured out milk and oil and then added the eggs. These were difficult things for him to talk about, but because it was important to Patience, he forced himself to elaborate. "Money was never really an issue. Happiness was. He often indicated to me that he felt trapped. That he wished he hadn't gone into business for himself. He wanted me to have more choices, more freedom, and he urged me to go far away to school, to spread my wings and not return to the South or the shackles that he had made for himself in trying to be independently successful in a dog-eat-dog world."

Her eyes widened in surprise. "He didn't want you to take over his business?"

"No," Josh said harshly, remembering that for a very long time he hadn't understood that, either.

Patience washed an apple and a handful of grapes while Josh stirred the egg mixture. "Did you have any brothers or sisters?"

Josh shook his head. "It was just my dad and me."

"Then there must have been some degree of closeness, if it was just the two of you."

"I wish that had been the case," Josh admitted as he measured baking powder, salt and flour into a bowl, relying on memory rather than any written recipe. "But my dad was a pretty moody guy. He was often depressed, and when he was he wouldn't talk about it or let me help him. And he constantly impressed upon me that a single moment of weakness could ruin my whole life."

Patience made a clucking sound as she got out some peaches and cantaloupe to add to the grapes and apple she had sliced into the bowl. "That does sound grim," she sympathized.

"It often was." Josh brought out an electric waffle iron he had spotted earlier, opened it and sprayed it with no-stick cooking spray. "I wish we could have fixed that somehow, but we never did, and when my dad died, we were still more or less estranged," he related sadly. "Speaking to each other, but not close. Not the way I always wanted to be, the way I had once been to my mother."

"I've never thought about it, but I guess I was lucky to have my brothers and Uncle Max when my parents died. It wasn't the same without my parents, of course. It could never be the same. But we still were a family," Patience finished passionately.

And for a woman like Patience, family was everything, Josh thought. "Max told me some stories from when you were kids." He went to turn the sizzling bacon.

She smiled at the mention of Max, already looking a little embarrassed. "Such as . . . ?"

Josh grinned, delighted to be able to tease her a little again. "The time Trace was trying to teach you how to cast a fishing rod, and he got so caught up in demonstrating the proper method and wouldn't let you do it."

Patience chuckled. "I got tired of waiting around and ended up knocking us both into the stream."

Josh laughed. Her version matched Max's exactly.

"What else?" Patience prodded him on enthusiastically, while outside the rain began to come down in torrents against the side of the log cabin.

Figuring they would be up awhile, Josh put on some coffee, too. "He told me you used to read to Cody all the time when he was younger, that between the two of you you went through the entire Hardy Boys series. And all of the Nancy Drew books, too."

"What can I say?" Patience added fresh pineapple to the bowl and stirred it gently. "We were both hooked on mysteries, and those books were very big at the time."

"It must have been nice having siblings," Josh said enviously as he plugged in the waffle iron. "You don't know how many times I've wished for the same."

Patience smiled, a little shyly, then was silent a moment, looking almost wistful again. "Do you want more than one child?" she asked softly.

Josh looked at Patience and knew she was the woman of his dreams. "I want a houseful of them," he confided happily.

"Me, too." Patience gave a soft, satisfied sigh. "Boys or girls?"

Josh shrugged and took her into his arms. "It doesn't matter," he replied, looking down at her as the storm raged overhead. "As long as I have a big, loving, rowdy family with the kind of deep and lasting love you McKendricks seem to have for each other, I'll be happy."

Patience toyed with a button on his shirt. He could feel the contentment flowing through her. It was enough to induce him to confide, "Mostly, I just want to be there for my kids, in the way my own dad wasn't." He pushed away the pain and the memories, tightening his hold on her and the present. The promise of the future loomed closer and more enticing than ever. "I want them to know they can come to me with any question and any problem and know I'll be there for them, always."

Patience looked up at him with shining eyes. "Sounds like we have the same view and standards when it comes to parenting."

Yes, they did. "Which was maybe why Max paired us," Josh mused out loud.

"Maybe." Patience paused. "I just have one more question," she said quietly, the troubled light coming back into her eyes again without warning. "Do you know anything about Alec's childhood?"

FOR A MOMENT, Josh looked as if she had jabbed him in the gut, and she could have shot herself for asking. Yet she knew it was part of the mystery of Alec's leaving her so inexplicably, and she had to understand that fully before she was going to be free to love again, the way Josh wanted her to love him.

He dropped his arms and moved away. "Alec never talked about that. To me or anyone else, at least not that I know of."

His back to her, he removed the skillet from the stove and lifted the bacon out of the pan to drain.

Patience knew that was true. "You're right, he didn't," she said, refusing to give up on her search for the truth. Hands folded in front of her, she continued watching Josh carefully. "I've always wondered why."

Josh shrugged and wouldn't look at her. "I guess we'll never know," he said at last.

To him, Patience thought, frustrated, it was a closed book. And maybe, she realized, that was the way it should be. She had loved Alec and loved him deeply. But if she was honest, she would have to admit that there had been problems from the very beginning of her relationship with Alec. He had never once opened up to her about his early life the way Josh just had. There'd been passion, but no true intimacy. And without that, what kind of a relationship, never mind marriage, would she and Alec have had? Certainly not a satisfying one.

Maybe everyone was right, Patience thought wearily. Maybe it was time for her to let go of the past, once and for all. Particularly since she had a chance to have the child she had always wanted with Josh. And a love affair, too.

"You okay?" Josh asked finally.

Patience nodded. She turned her attention back to Josh's cooking and saw he had poured batter into the waffle iron. She watched as he shut the lid and set the timer on it. "You really seem to know what you're doing," she said.

Josh grinned. "Breakfast is the one meal I really know how to cook. And eat."

He wasn't alone in that, Patience thought. Alec had also liked to eat eggs and pancakes at night. And he'd often had pizza for breakfast.

And that made her think about the very first time they'd gone anywhere together. It had been after class.

"WANT TO GET something to eat?" the sandy-haired *young man with the serious expression and wire-rimmed glasses asked.*

Patience smiled as she shifted the books in her arms a little closer to her chest. She had been hoping Alec Vaughn would notice her. She had hardly been able to concentrate during the entire freshman study session. He was so darn good-looking, but he hardly seemed to know it.

He fell into step beside her as they walked through the library doors and out into the brisk October evening. "I know it's kind of late," he continued a little shyly in his distinctive Southern drawl, "but there's a coffee shop

*a couple blocks from here that's open all night. So if
you aren't too sleepy, I'd be grateful for the company."*

"Sure. Sounds good. I could go for a cup of hot cocoa and some cinnamon toast," Patience said, stepping a little closer to his tall, rangy frame.

"Me now, I could go for some Belgian waffles with maple butter," Alec said softly. He shook his head at her in a teasing manner. "Can't have waffles without maple butter...."

"I DON'T SUPPOSE there's any maple butter in here," Josh said, searching the refrigerator.

"What?" Patience asked, dragged from her memories back into the present. She couldn't have heard right.

"Never mind. I can make some up."

She watched, stunned, as Josh got out the butter and maple syrup. It was a coincidence, she told herself firmly. It had to be.   But what if it wasn't? What if she'd just been made the biggest fool of all? A chill of uneasiness slid down her spine and her insides twisted into knots.

"It'd be better if we had maple extract," he said casually, "but this'll do. All we have to do is add a little syrup to the butter and—" He paused, having picked up on the way she was staring at him. To her irritation, he obviously didn't have a clue why.

"Patience? What's wrong?"

Chapter Ten

Dear Patience,
What should I do with a rowdy, uncooperative beau?

Sincerely,
Ridden Roughshod in Rio

Dear Ridden Roughshod in Rio,
Every stallion needs to get used to the saddle sometime. Throw that bridle on and tame him, honey.

Patience

"Alec liked to eat pancakes or waffles with maple butter, especially late in the evening."

"So what are you saying, Patience?" Josh sounded both shocked and appalled. "That now you want me not just to remind you of Alec but to actually be him?"

The way Josh said that made her feel ridiculous. She squared her shoulders and faced him defiantly. "No, of course not."

"Then what is this about?" The dangerous glint was back in Josh's eyes.

She hesitated a moment, not sure if she was imagining things or not, then decided to go for broke. "I just find it odd you have a passion for maple butter, too, that's all," she said coolly.

He shot her a sharp look. She knew that he wanted her to back off, which was exactly why she couldn't. Because like it or not, Alec and Josh did share an ability to kiss her senseless, and she had never, in her entire life, met anyone else who could do that to her. So there had to be some tie there. Something along the lines of whatever it was that Holly Diehl had been hinting at earlier. Maybe the two men were related. Physically related. Brothers or cousins, perhaps?

"And odder still that we both seemed enamored of you?" Josh guessed after a moment, having picked up on her suspiciousness.

Patience worked to quell her racing pulse. "Maybe," she flung back, and found the more excited and upset she got, the calmer he was.

"Only there's a difference." Josh removed the first batch of waffles from the iron and slid them onto a plate.

Patience watched him add a second layer of batter to the iron and shut the lid with the ease of someone who had spent years cooking for himself. "Really, what?"

Josh wiped his hands on a towel, turned toward her and took her into his arms. His mouth curved briefly as he looked down at her. "I won't be standing you up at the altar tomorrow. When it's time for us to get married, I'll be there."

Patience laid a hand on his chest, creating as much distance as she could between them. She knew if he kissed her again she would be tempted just to forget everything. "I haven't definitely decided to go through with it myself yet," she warned.

Unperturbed by her announcement, he stroked his hand down her face. She could tell by the darkening of his eyes he was thinking about the incredibly passionate way they had made love earlier. "But you want to, don't you?" he stated softly.

Patience hauled in a shaky breath. She wanted to approach this engagement and wedding of theirs with the kind of gut-level practicality and common sense she had not exercised in her previous engagement to Alec. "Wanting something and actually doing it are two different things." How well she knew that! "I want to honor my Uncle Max's wishes and I want a baby, a family, to make my life complete. But I also know I will never be happy with less than the complete package, and I can't and won't get married just for the sake of getting married."

"Or just to have a child," he qualified.

Patience nodded slowly. "If nothing else, the past thirty hours have shown me I have to have it all."

"I'm willing to try to achieve that, if you are."

Against all common sense, Patience was tempted. And she knew she shouldn't be. "Part of me even thinks I should run now," she admitted with gut-wrenching honesty.

This did not seem to surprise him. "Because of the closeness we've already achieved," he guessed.

And the fact I'm still not sure I can trust you. "Yes."

His eyes darkened with turbulent emotion. "What if we've already made a baby?"

Then part of me will rejoice, and the other part will be scared to death. Careful to keep her emotions under wraps lest she become even more vulnerable where he was concerned, she replied, "If I am pregnant—" as we both suspect I might be "—then it becomes a lot more complicated."

"To the point where you are going to need me," he said firmly as the timer on the iron went off, signaling the waffles were done.

As she watched him tend to their supper, Patience wondered how she could have thought, even for a second, that Josh and Alec were the same man. When it came right down to it, the two were nothing alike. And it was more than just their looks or their physiques. Josh understood things about her that Alec never would have. Josh went after things with a ruthless single-mindedness that Alec had just not possessed.

As they sat down to eat, she told Josh bluntly, "We can't get married just because I might be pregnant. Or even because we both want to have a child."

He inclined his head in obvious disagreement and pinned her with a look. "I've heard worse reasons for couples getting together."

Patience took a bite of her waffle. "We're not other couples. We're us. And we've been foolish, Josh," she said with a weary sigh. "Very foolish."

He lifted his gaze to hers. "Nevertheless, every child needs two parents whenever possible. And we'll find a way to work it out," he said with a quiet confidence that implied that together they could handle anything that came their way. "Whether we are married or not, or lovers or not." He covered her hand with his own. "We'll do it for our baby."

His comments hit home, forcing Patience to think about how hard it had been for her when her parents had died in the earthquake. Uncle Max had done his best, and he had filled her father's shoes admirably, but he had never been able to do the things her mother would have done for them.

Her brothers had seemed to cope with that better than she had, maybe because they were guys. But she had suffered from the lack of feminine advice on a variety of subjects and privately felt her broken engagement to Alec was proof of that.

''Well?'' Josh prodded as she looked down at their entwined fingers.

Deep down, Patience realized she would not want to deprive her baby of a father any more than she wanted to deprive herself of a baby.

His confidence in them as a couple was catching. A slow smile spread across her face. ''Well, Uncle Max did advise me to dance with the one who brung me,'' Patience said, grinning.

''He advised us both that,'' Josh concurred.

Which meant they should appreciate the one they were with, in this case each other, Patience thought, instead of always wishing for what once was or could have been. Hadn't she done that for too many years already?

Josh pushed back his chair. ''So maybe we should throw caution to the wind this once and follow Max's wishes for us.'' Taking her hand, he tugged her to her feet and drew her into his arms.

''And do what?'' Patience asked as Josh's lips lowered slowly, inexorably to hers.

''Make a go of it,'' he said, kissing her deeply. ''Not just for now, but forever.''

PATIENCE CLUNG TO JOSH as he carried her up the stairs and into the master bedroom. ''Feeling a little reckless tonight?'' she teased as he lowered her gently to the mattress and followed her down onto the rumpled covers of the bed. She had to admit she was glad he was. For she was feeling reckless, too.

He unbuttoned her blouse at record speed. His eyes were dark with love and longing. And though he hadn't yet said the words to her—might never say the words—she felt them in her heart. "You inspire me," he murmured, exploring the curves of her breasts with his lips and hands, then he straightened so Patience could help him off with his shirt, too.

Her heart racing, she smoothed her hands across the brawny width of his shoulders and down his muscular chest. Smart or not, she found him irresistible. "Truth be told," she said softly, "you inspire me, too."

Together, they kicked off their jeans. Patience was filled with the warmth of anticipation. "We're dangerous together."

"It would seem so," Josh murmured as they helped each other dispense with their remaining clothing. When they were naked, he took her into his arms and rolled so she was beneath him. With both hands, he brushed the hair from her face. "Regrets?"

"No," she whispered, meaning it with all her heart even as she marveled over the wonder of finding him at all. "Well," she amended mischievously after a moment as he worked his way down her throat, past her collarbone to the curve of her breast, "maybe one."

Stunned, Josh lifted his head. Seeing she was teasing, he grinned. "What?"

Patience smiled as she rested her hands on his shoulders, then worked them all the way down his chest; she loved the smoothness of his skin beneath the mat of dark, downy hair. "That we didn't get around to this sooner. Think of all the time we wasted."

"Hmmm." Josh went back to nuzzling her neck with single-minded devotion, tantalizing deftly even as he explored. "A whole... what was it... twenty-two hours?"

"Something like that, yes." Patience gasped and arched her back as his teeth worried the sensitive lobe of her ear. She wanted to learn and experience every inch of him. She wanted him in her life. And she knew, if they tried hard enough, they could find a way to make everything work. And she sensed he knew it, too.

He warned, only half teasing, "We're going to have to make up for the lost time, you know." Then he kissed her again, deeply, reverently this time, until she was weak with longing, dizzy with desire.

Patience trembled as he slid a hand between her legs and found her sensitive core. She wanted him across her, covering her with his heat and his weight. "I know," she said as she closed her hand around him, all of her waiting for all of him. She pressed herself close and touched her lips to his, whispering, "I'm looking forward to it."

PATIENCE SNUGGLED against Josh as the storm continued to rage outside. "What are you thinking?" He stroked her hair tenderly.

Enveloped in the warmth of him, her body still humming contentedly with the aftershocks of their lovemaking, Patience cuddled close. It was odd. Many of her questions were still unanswered, but she had never been happier than she was at that moment. She had the feeling Josh felt that way, too. "That no one has ever been able to make me feel the way you do." *That for the first time in my life I am so close to having everything I've ever dreamed of having.*

Josh pressed a kiss on her temple and stroked a questing hand toward her back. Murmuring her pleasure, she surged against him, the softness of her body sliding across the hardness of his. She felt the response of his body and knew he wanted to make love to her again. "You are one incredible woman, Patience McKendrick," he said softly.

They kissed again, only to be interrupted by a brilliant flash of light and, one second later, a deafening clap of thunder that made them both jump. Patience shuddered as they drew apart. "Gosh, that was close!" she said.

Another flash of lightning followed. Only this time as the thunder roared, the lights went out and stayed out.

WITHOUT POWER, the house was pitch-black and deadly silent, except for the staccato sound of the rain pounding against the roof and windows.

Swearing about the occasional inconveniences of living so far out in the country and having aboveground utilities to boot, Patience reached across Josh, groping for the phone. She pulled it into bed, punched in a few buttons, then held it to her ear. Immediately, she muttered her displeasure. "Problem?" Josh asked as Patience grappled with the bedside table and came up with a flashlight, which she immediately switched on.

"The phone is dead, too. Since we have aboveground utilities this far out, when the electricity gets knocked out by a storm, often the phone service does, as well. Naturally, that makes it a little hard to report it, especially since our cell phone won't work in storms, either."

"We've got a shortwave radio out in the ranch office next to the barns," Josh suggested. He peered out the window. In the distance, he could see people coming out of the bunkhouse, flashlights in hand. He was already reaching for his jeans. "I'll go ask one of the hired hands to notify the power and phone companies that our lines are down." Pausing long enough to kiss her, he reasoned, "Good thing we have one more thirty-minute break left."

Patience started to get up. "I can go with you."

"No. It's best you stay here," Josh said. "There's no use both of us getting soaked to the skin and the rain is still coming down pretty hard, and at an angle." He whistled for Goldie. She came running.

"Stay with Patience," he instructed his dog. He turned to Patience. "She'll watch over you."

Patience smiled, snuggling deeper under the covers. "Or vice versa."

Josh grabbed his hat and jacket and headed out the door. No sooner had he shut the front door behind him than someone came out of the shadows. She had a long yellow rain slicker on, the kind all the ranchers wore. The collar was pulled up against her face, the Stetson low across her brow. He still recognized her immediately. It wasn't a good feeling, knowing she had used this opportunity to see him.

"Holly."

She stepped beneath the overhang. "We need to talk." She glanced furtively at the house. "Where is Patience?"

"Inside." And Josh thanked his lucky stars for that.

"Any chance of her coming down to join us?" Holly demanded, darting another look at the still, dark house.

Josh thought of Patience snuggled beneath the covers upstairs, sleepy and replete from their lovemaking. Lovemaking he wanted nothing more than to continue throughout the night. "No, she will not come down here." With a scowl, he demanded irritably, "What are you doing out here?" Holly's showing up like this, shadowing him constantly, reminded him of the days he had lived with her. No matter how much everyone had told him it was for his own good, he had still felt like a prisoner then, and he was beginning to feel imprisoned now, both by his memories and all he couldn't and would not ever share with Patience.

"Three guesses," Holly said with a disgruntled sigh that let him know this was not her choice, either. And suddenly Josh knew. Patience had been in her study a long time earlier this evening, and not just with her brother Cody, who had dropped by at one point for a brief, private chat.

"Patience did something?"

"You might say that," Holly replied sourly, pulling the brim of her rain-soaked hat even lower across her brow. "She E-mailed a request for information on the death of Alec Vaughn, his father and anything on mob activity in the Yale area at the same time. Fortunately, we were able to intercept her request before it reached her newspaper data bank, but we figure it's only a matter of time before she checks her computer again and figures out that the request was not received."

"Or figures out she's looking at mob activity in the wrong area of the country," Josh theorized grimly.

"That, too."

"Oh, and one other thing. She decided to investigate me, too," Holly stated unhappily.

Josh swore silently. He had been afraid of this. Patience was as curious as the day was long. Worse, she was a journalist, which meant she knew how to research and had the resources to do so. "What do you want me to do?" he asked gruffly.

Holly winced as the wind picked up to even stronger gusts. "I want you to either get Patience McKendrick to back off, or move on."

"Some choice," Josh scoffed. "I can tell Patience everything and put her in permanent danger, or I can leave inexplicably and break her heart, in which case she would probably never recover, marry, or have a child." He couldn't bear to see that happen.

Holly folded her arms in front of her and fumed. "I warned you not to come here, Josh. I told you it could only lead to heartbreak, yours and hers."

Josh stared at the lightning flashing across the sky. The storm seemed to be reaching behemoth heights, he thought as the next clap of thunder reverberated loudly throughout the black night sky. "You know why I had to do it," he said tersely. It had been the only way either he or Patience would ever have had any peace. It was the only way to put Alec's death and disappearance from her life behind them.

"I know," Holly said, for a moment looking almost sympathetic to his plight. "I even understand, Josh, but that doesn't change anything. You still have a choice to make. *And like it or not, it has to be made now, before any more damage is done.*"

PATIENCE WAS DRESSED by the time Josh came back inside. Flashlight in hand, she had been getting ready to go out and look for him. It was good she hadn't had to go, she thought, because he was drenched to the skin.

"Did you get on the shortwave and request to have the power and phone service restored?" She grabbed a towel from the upstairs linen closet and gently blotted the moisture dripping from his hair onto his face and neck.

Josh shook his head, his expression so grim it alarmed her. "Not yet," he said quietly as her heart skipped a beat.

Patience swallowed. "Then what were you doing all this time?" she asked.

Josh shrugged, looking for a moment as if he didn't even know where to begin.

Patience's inner warning system went on red alert. "What is it?" she asked softly. "Josh, you can tell me anything."

He hesitated in the act of unbuttoning his soaked western shirt.

Patience began to get even more scared. "Josh—"

He laid a hand across her shoulder. "We have to talk."

Patience began to help him with his shirt. "Okay, but first let's get you out of these clothes."

"No," Josh said in a voice that was so unexpectedly harsh it alarmed her. He turned tortured eyes to hers. "I have to say this and get it over with."

Patience's stomach knotted up. "Okay."

"You know it's been years since I've let myself get really close to anyone."

She nodded, panicking inwardly, but said calmly, "I gathered as much."

He swallowed. "There's a reason I haven't been able to be completely honest with you."

Patience was beginning to think that maybe she did not want to hear this from him. "So what are you telling me?'' she joked lamely. ''That you're some sort of federal agent here on a sting operation?''

To her surprise, Josh winced. ''Not exactly.''

At the seriousness in his low tone, the laughter vanished from her eyes, the happiness from her heart. And suddenly she knew that whatever he was, he was not a law officer. ''Josh—''

He held up a hand, stopping her before she could go on. ''I haven't committed a crime,'' he told her soberly. ''So you needn't worry about that.''

Patience gave a shaky sigh of relief. ''That's good to hear.''

Josh wrapped a comforting arm around her shoulders. ''Everything I've done, I've done to protect you. I didn't want you to carry the burden of fear and tension I've carried all these years and am just now beginning to shed.''

''That's good, too,'' she murmured, unable to shake the feeling that whatever it was he was about to tell her could easily destroy them both.

Before Josh could say anything else, another flash of lightning forked across the sky, accompanied by a simultaneous crack of thunder so loud it had them both starting and instinctively ducking for cover. When they rose slowly and looked out the window, they saw it wasn't the studio that had been hit but the foaling barn housing Mandy and her newborn foal, Impatience.

FLAMES CRACKLED from the top of the barn, undiminished by the pouring rain. Fear raced through Patience. ''Josh, that's the barn where Mandy and her foal are!'' she cried.

''I'll get them out.''

With no regard for his own safety, he dashed across the yard in the pouring rain, Patience hard on his heels. Acrid smoke rolled from the jagged opening in the roof of the barn. The sounds of the mares and foals whinnying in terror filled the barn. In the distance, the hands were beginning to straggle out of the bunkhouse. Patience and Josh were much closer.

"Stay outside! I'll go in," Josh said as the entire roof of the foaling barn caught and flamed.

"No! We'll never get all the mares and their foals out if I don't help!" Patience pushed past Josh's restraining arm, and, head down, stormed deeper into the barn.

Together, they reached Mandy's stall. Impatience was at the rear, cowering and mewling in terror. Mandy was kicking furiously at the front, trying to break through the wood.

Josh used calming words to put her at ease as red-hot cinders poured down on them from overhead. He unlatched the stall. Mandy came barreling out, then reared again, whinnying in terror.

Josh caught her by the bridle, and covering her eyes with a cloth, he jerked her toward the entrance of the barn. As Mandy headed toward the exit, Patience took over while Josh went back to get the quivering foal. Coughing and choking on the smoke, he gathered the foal up into his arms and followed Patience and Mandy out of the barn.

Again and again, they went back inside. The hands raced to join them. Finally, all the animals were out— just as the sides of the barn were swept into the flames.

IT WAS A GOOD TWO HOURS before they were sure all the fires were out. And though they were fortunate enough to get all their horses out intact, in the interim, five of the ten barns had caught fire, too, and suffered some sort of damage.

Soaring Eagle and the hired hands helped Josh and Patience resettle all the horses in new quarters. Exhausted, Patience and Josh returned to the main house. Both were drenched, exhausted and covered with soot.

"The power is still off," Josh said, frowning.

"At this point, I'll settle for a cold shower and some clean, dry clothes," Patience said wearily.

"I'll build a fire in the hearth," Josh said.

He was as good as his word. When she came back downstairs after her cold shower, wrapped in a warm, terry cloth robe, he went up to take his turn.

Patience had an Irish coffee waiting for Josh when he rejoined her in front of the hearth. It was four in the morning. The thunderstorm had passed but the rain continued its steady drumming on the roof. Patience knew there would be much to do the following morning, repairing the damage and cleaning up after the storm, and that she would be required to help. Nevertheless, sleep seemed miles away. "I don't know about you," she confided with a winning smile, "but I am still way too keyed up to sleep."

Clad in jeans and an unbuttoned shirt, Josh joined her on the sofa. "The Irish coffee should help."

"Eventually, the fatigue has to set in." Patience stared at the fireplace. "Can you believe we're getting married in just twelve hours?" she murmured.

WERE THEY? JOSH WONDERED. Especially when she heard what he had to tell her. Would she still feel the way she had?

"Of course our inheritance has been damaged somewhat," Patience continued.

Josh touched her hand, loving the softness and the strength. "But you're safe." For that he was very grateful.

Patience smiled. "And so are you."

Josh's throat tightened and he shook his head. "When you dashed into that barn ahead of me—"

"I know," Patience concurred, resting her hand over his. "I knew I could lose you, too. But we did the right thing. All the horses are safe. And the barns that were damaged can be repaired. The storm is finally even letting up."

Or was it just beginning? Josh wondered.

Patience took the edge of the towel she had roped around her neck and rubbed it through the dampness of her just combed hair. "Before the fire, you were going to tell me something." She paused. "What was it?"

Chapter Eleven

Dear Patience,
He says he has changed, but I'm wondering. Should I forgive a man who once heartlessly walked out on me?

> Sincerely,
> Abandoned in Amarillo

Dear Abandoned in Amarillo,
Never! Or in the words of someone much wiser: Fool me once, shame on you. Fool me twice, shame on me.

> As Cautious as a She-Bear with Cubs,
> Patience

Josh took a deep breath, wishing it had not come to this. "I've lied to you, if not directly, then by omission."

Patience dropped the comb she had been holding. She stared at him, her hands lying limply in her lap. "What are you talking about?"

She looked so hurt, it was all Josh could do to go on. "I am who you think I am, but I'm someone else, too."

Patience went completely still. "What are you trying to tell me?" she asked hoarsely.

"That I have another identity, one I've been keeping from you."

At the low urgency in his tone, some of the happiness left her eyes. She backed away to the other end of the sofa and sat with her legs tucked up close to her body, the edges of her robe drawn tightly down to her ankles. Her spine stiffened, and she looked as if she were bracing herself for the worst. "I don't think I want to hear this," she said quietly.

Josh put his untouched coffee aside. He would have given anything if he did not have to do this, but Patience had given him no choice. "I'm Alec Vaughn." He took one of her ice-cold hands in his and clasped it warmly. "I'm the man you fell in love with."

It took a moment for his words to sink in. When they did, she shook off his touch and stumbled abruptly to her feet. Her eyes still on him, she backed to the fireplace. She was white as a sheet and trembling visibly. "What kind of sick joke is this?"

Josh stood, too. Knowing even if she didn't that she needed him to hold her, he started toward her slowly. "It's not a joke. Believe me," he said with heartfelt regret, keeping his eyes on her pale face, "I wish it were."

She blinked, still appearing to be in shock. "You didn't die—" she murmured, confused. "But—" She gestured inanely, her hands trembling all the more. "The obit in the newspaper, the one Uncle Max dug up—"

"Was a fake, planted to make people think I had died."

He started to take her in his arms, but she motioned him away with short, choppy gestures. "And you went along with it?" She stared at him incredulously.

Guilt flooded him anew. And regret that he'd had to hurt her, ever. "Yes."

Cheeks pinkening, she released a short, bitter laugh. "And you let everyone believe you were dead all this time!" She stared at him, enraged.

"I was—am. At least Alec is." Josh tried to get close to her, to take her in his arms again, but again she held him off and backed away.

"I'm in the federal witness protection program."

She stared at him, as if unsure whether to believe him or not. Considering all he had thrown at her, he could hardly blame her for her distrust of him, yet it saddened him deeply nonetheless.

"Why?" she asked finally, still eyeing him uncertainly.

Josh returned to the sofa and sat down on the edge of it. He lifted his eyes to hers and, trying to make this as easy for her as possible, said gently, "You remember when we were planning the wedding, and your Uncle Max and my father both refused to attend?"

Patience nodded slowly. Her blue eyes shimmering with hurt, she elaborated cautiously, "Because they thought we were too young."

Josh nodded, remembering. "I couldn't bear seeing you that upset, so I decided the only thing to do was to get home and make sure that at least one of our parents—in this case my father—showed up for the wedding. So I told my roommate, William, I had an errand to run and caught a flight home the day before we were to get married. Figuring my father would try and talk me out of going to see him in person, I didn't tell him I was coming. I just showed up. Only when I got there, my dad wasn't alone." Josh paused, his stomach knotting at the memory. "He was with a couple of thugs. They were trying to make him get the goods on one of his friends, a fellow businessman."

Josh kneaded the tense muscles at the back of his neck. "Apparently all the businessmen in the area had been laundering money for the mob for years. But the Feds were getting close, and the IRS was breathing down their necks. The guy who owned the café next to my father's dry-cleaning business had just been audited, and although the Feds hadn't yet been able to prove what he and the others had been doing, he was scared. The mob suspected he was close to turning informant, and as I found out later from Holly Diehl, they were right. The mob wanted my father, who was a trusted friend, to lure this guy away on a fishing expedition, find out for the mob what—if any—deal had been made with the Feds, and then make sure his friend had an unfortunate accident while they were out at sea. My father refused to be part of any murder, and that's when they started beating him. I tried to intervene. But I was unarmed, and at that point in my life no competition for guys who made their living with clubs and brass knuckles, beating the stuffing out of people." Josh grimaced at the memory of the savage beating he had taken. "They pounded the hell out of my face, probably so I'd be unrecognizable if I was found. Then they broke one elbow, my collarbone, and smashed one of my knees."

Patience stared at him in shock. "That's where you got all the scars," she said slowly.

Josh nodded. "And why I look and seem so different to you now, because once I recovered, I worked out and learned how to fight."

"You used to wear glasses—"

"For a while I wore contacts, then when it became available, I had corrective surgery on my eyes. Now I no longer need to wear corrective lenses of any kind."

Still struggling to take everything in, Patience edged back toward the sofa and perched on the end of it. Hugging her arms close to her chest, she tucked her legs beneath her and asked shakily, "Your father got the same treatment as you, I guess?"

A lump in his throat, Josh nodded. He still wished he had been able to make peace with his father, to do something—anything—to save him. Aware Patience was waiting to hear the rest of his story, he forced himself to continue, his voice hardening. "They threw us in the back of this van and drove us out of New Orleans, and to make the identification of the bodies and prosecution more difficult, over the state line to some remote area in Mississippi." Tears stung Josh's eyes. "My father had totally lost consciousness by then, so I don't think he was aware when they took him out of the van and put him behind the wheel of his own car."

Patience was white as a sheet. She stared at him, her heart going out to him. "But you knew—" she guessed in a choked voice.

Josh nodded, comforted by the aching sympathy in her eyes. "But with my broken bones, there wasn't much I could do about it. As soon as we were in the car, they shifted it into drive and shoved us over the cliff." He shuddered and closed his eyes against the grisly images flashing in his head. Feeling suddenly, unbearably weary, he dropped back against the sofa cushions and forced himself to finish his story. "My memories after that are kind of piecemeal. I remember the way the car turned end over end, the blackness of the night, and then the next thing I knew I woke up some distance away from the car. I had glass all over me, but I was alive." He paused, shaking his head in sadness and regret, then pushed on grimly. "My father wasn't so lucky. He burned to death in the car."

"Oh, Josh…" Tears flowed down Patience's cheeks. She reached over and held his hand tightly.

Basking in the comfort she offered, Josh went on. "I was able to tell the local authorities what had happened and they immediately had me in protective custody. To protect me and throw off the crooks, they ran stories of a car accident in rural Mississippi where two John Does had died. They had no idea who the two men inside the car were, only that it had gone off a cliff and the two men inside had been burned beyond recognition."

"Surely someone back in New Orleans knew you and your father were missing—"

"The mob took care of all that, too. They brought in a moving van the next day, cleaned out all our belongings. They told everyone in the community that my father's business had sold and we'd both relocated somewhere out of the country to avoid paying taxes on the profit. All traces of us ever living there were wiped out."

"So the mob thought you and your father were both dead."

"They were sure of it," Josh confirmed. "And that misconception on their part is the only thing that saved my life."

A silence fell between them. Josh could tell she was still struggling to take it all in. "I was told that contacting you or anyone in my life was out of the question until after the trial. So I spent the next five years in hiding, with Holly Diehl and a host of other agents watching over me." Josh grimaced, recalling those lonely years. "Once the trial was over and the crooks locked up, they put me in the witness protection program and I started all over again."

The color was coming back into Patience's cheeks. "And that's why you never showed up at the wedding," she said after a moment. "Why you never called or let me know what was happening."

It had not been his choice, but he had done it because he had to. "I couldn't, not without putting you in danger or taking you into hiding with me," Josh explained.

Patience jerked her hand away from his furiously and replied in a voice that was icy with disdain, "So you chose to break my heart instead?"

"What choice did I have?" Josh shot back calmly, as if he had done the right thing instead of damn near destroying her, Patience thought. "I didn't want you to have to live the kind of life I was living."

She glared at him as she uncurled her legs and vaulted to her feet. "Are you sure you didn't just see your way out and take it?"

Josh drew a long breath and kept his eyes firmly on hers. He had to make her understand, no matter what it took. "I loved you. I still love you," he said firmly.

"But not enough to be honest with me then," Patience retorted bitterly as tears flowed from her eyes in a blinding torrent of hurt. "Not enough to tell me who you were now, right from the start," she added with a short, harsh laugh.

Josh was aware she was on the verge of becoming hysterical.

"Instead, you made me think I was losing my mind, thinking of Alec so incessantly and seeing flashes of him in you."

He closed the distance between them and touched her shoulder gently. "That wasn't my intention at all."

She skirted away from him, and he knew in a glance that she was never going to forgive him for this. Never. She shoved her trembling hands deep into the pockets of her thick terry cloth robe. "Then why did you come here?" she demanded.

His gray eyes grew even sadder. "A lot of reasons."

Her limbs seemed so stiff and heavy that Patience felt as though she had been carved out of stone. "I'm listening."

His tone softened persuasively. He looked at her as if begging her to let go of her anger and understand, to see things from his point of view. "The two of us had never had any real closure. I knew how much I had changed—especially physically. I thought—hoped—if I saw you again, or at least found out how you were doing, that I might be able to go on with my life."

Go on with his life. His words hit her like a hammer blow. *He had come here not intending to bed her again, not to love her or rescue her, but to leave.*

"So why didn't you do just that, get what you needed and go?" she asked coldly, feeling her heart turn to stone, too.

Josh's eyes darkened protectively. "Because you weren't all right. At least not in Max's mind. Or anyone else's."

Patience did not want to think about the long, lonely years she had spent mourning Alec. Or the fool Josh had made of her once again. When was she going to learn not to trust her instincts? "Surely the fact I'm a syndicated columnist and a public figure in my own right counts for something," she said, beginning to pace again.

"Maybe more than you know." Josh lifted the coffeepot from the warmer near the fire. He freshened her coffee and held it out for her. She refused with a shake of her head and brushed on by. He caught up with her and pushed it into her hands anyway.

Mission accomplished, he backed off. With a steady confidence that made her want to toss something at his head, he continued, "I'd been reading your column, and I just couldn't reconcile the sweet and trusting girl you had once been with the tart-tongued cynic in your columns."

"Well, they are one and the same," Patience snapped. Because she was so upset she felt as if she were going to explode, she decided to down the whiskey-and-cream-laced brew anyway.

He watched her with a smug look. "And that should tell you something, just like the fact you and I both are still single tells me something."

Patience glanced at the ceiling in silent supplication, then turned back to him. "I am single because I haven't wanted to get married," she told him stiffly as she set her glass down on the table with a resounding clink.

To her increasing irritation, Josh made no immediate comment about that. Instead, he leaned against the fireplace, his shirt still open to the waist. Barefoot, his jeans clinging to his long, muscular legs, he had never looked sexier nor more approachable than he did at that moment. And that irritated her immensely. She did not want to be noticing how good he smelled—like soap and English Leather. Didn't want to notice that despite the blackout and the barn fire, he had still taken the time to shave again. For her. Because he wanted to make love to her again.

"Haven't wanted to get married or haven't found the right man?" Josh prodded finally, his eyes traveling over her languorously, as if the outcome of this battle they were waging had already been decided, the war already won.

Despite her promise to stay mad at him forever, Patience felt the ice around her heart thaw a little. For a man who had been out of her life for seventeen years, he was awfully hard to discourage now. Which was even more confusing, because she knew he was there at great personal risk.

"What's the difference?" she retorted, glowering at him. For the hell of it, she added another dash of Irish whiskey to her coffee and downed it in a single gulp. "I'm happy enough."

Half of Josh's mouth curved up in obvious disagreement with her assessment. "Your Uncle Max didn't think so." He pushed away from the fireplace and sauntered toward her lazily. "As it happens, Patience, he was damn worried about you."

Patience hesitated. "He told you that?" she asked, regretting that she might have caused her late uncle a moment's worry.

"Not in so many words, not at first," Josh confided. He continued to close the distance between them, not stopping until they were mere inches apart. "But it was no secret with the hired hands that he had longed to see you settled down by now.''

Unfortunately, Patience knew that was true. Uncle Max had worried about her and blamed himself for her self-imposed solitude for years now. ''Did he know who you were?'' she asked quietly.

Josh braced his hands on the bare skin of his waist and shrugged. ''If he did, he never let on. As far as the past goes, I did what I thought was best.''

What he thought was best. How utterly arrogant. How utterly male. ''Without consulting me?'' Patience asked irately.

Josh sighed, beginning to look irritated now, too. ''I explained all that,'' he said with a thinly veiled tolerance that really grated on her nerves.

''Yes, I know.'' Patience spun away from him and moved so the cranberry red sofa was between them. ''I heard.''

He blew out a weary breath and raked both hands through the layers of his hair. ''How long are you going to stay angry with me about this?''

''I don't know,'' Patience replied cavalierly, tilting her chin at him. ''What sounds fair?'' she asked sweetly. ''Seventeen years? Or shall we go for twice that?'' Just to make sure he had suffered the way she had! And all for no reason, because she would have gone with him if only he had asked. Or never mind that, if he had simply told her he was in trouble!

''Patience—''

She glared at him, but her pique had absolutely no effect on him. He came toward her and held out his arms to her. She avoided him by stepping deftly around the sofa again, so it was still between them. As she faced off with him, her heart thudded with a telltale heaviness.

"Give me a break here, Patience. Give us both a break."

"You can't actually believe I would forgive you for something like this, can you?" she demanded, aware she was beginning to feel warm all over, whether from the potent Irish whiskey she had so swiftly imbibed or his increasingly audacious manner, she didn't know. She just knew he expected her to forgive him quickly and to make love now, and she had no intention of doing so.

Josh paused, a muscle working convulsively in his jaw. "I told you the truth!"

Careful to stay on the opposite side of the sofa from him, Patience resumed her pacing. "You did that because it was the only way to stop me from asking questions about Alec. If I hadn't been so curious, you never would have told me. Would you?"

Josh lifted his broad shoulders in an indolent shrug. To her frustration, he didn't deny it. "I admit I would have preferred to protect you," he said, as if keeping her in the dark and breaking her heart in the process were a completely laudable deed.

"And in the meantime do all my thinking, make all my decisions for me and completely shut me out of the process we call living a life!" Patience snapped back furiously.

Once again, he was silent, offering no defense except that he had loved her, then and now.

Drawing a ragged breath, Patience pushed on in a low voice barely above a whisper. "I'm a person, Josh. Alec...whoever you are. Flesh and blood. I have feelings, and a brain, and I want to be treated like the potential partner for life that I am, not just some...some ornamental child who needs your constant guidance and protection." She wanted him to need her the way she needed him.

Reaching over the back of the sofa, he grabbed her arm and hauled her toward him. "Do you think I wanted it this way?" Still hanging on to her tenaciously, he circled around the couch and caught her against him, length to length. "Damn it, Patience, I sacrificed my own happiness to protect you."

"And mine," she stormed, struggling unsuccessfully to be free of him. "And you know what hurts the most?" Giving in to her feelings, she pounded on his chest with her fists. "The fact you didn't even trust me enough to ask me what I wanted in all this. That you just decided for me." Just as Uncle Max had decided she shouldn't get married then, when she had wanted to, and that she should get married now, when she hadn't wanted to. She was so tired of people running her life for her.

He caught her wrists in a steely grip and kept them motionless against his chest. "I won't apologize for protecting you," Josh retorted stonily. "I did what I did to save your life. The mob would not have hesitated to go after you to get to me, Patience," he pointed out hoarsely.

"And now? What about now?" Patience demanded as the tears she had been holding back streamed down her face. "Are you in danger now that the thugs who killed your father are in jail?"

Josh softened his grip on her wrists but did not let her go. "I'll always be looking over my shoulder, I'll always be in danger. It's just a question of how much. As long as I'm Josh Colter, ranch veterinarian, as long as no one else connects me with Alec, I'm probably as safe as I'll ever be, right here and right now."

The thought of him in any kind of danger was enough to make her heart stop. And yet her anger, her hurt, remained at a completely unmanageable level. "So what are you saying?" Patience asked bitterly. "That had you only trusted me enough you could have told me who you were when I arrived at the ranch forty-some hours ago and we knew Max wanted us to be married?"

She waited for his answer, but it never came.

Instead, Josh said simply, "Would you have forgiven me if I had?"

Chapter Twelve

Dear Patience,
There's no denying it! I am unlucky in love. What
is a surefire way to change my luck?

Sincerely,
Gamblin' Gal

Dear Gamblin' Gal,
There is no such thing as being unlucky in love or
in life. People make their own luck. Get out there
and fix whatever's wrong, then try again.

Hopin' You Will Lasso Yourself Some Lovin',
Patience

That, Patience thought, was a hell of a question. "After seventeen long years of second-guessing myself and lamenting all we could have had and lost when you walked out on me, probably not," she said honestly.

Josh shrugged. "I rest my case."

Patience studied him. "You think I'm being unreasonable, don't you?"

Josh's glance narrowed derisively. "If the shoe fits . . ."

"You think I should just accept that you knew best then, just like you know best now, not just for you but for the both of us, and let that be the end of it?" she demanded hotly.

"Yes. I do."

She folded her arms in front of her and regarded him stormily. "Well, I don't." Spinning away from him, she started for the front hall.

Josh was hard on her heels. "Where are you going?"

Lifting the hem of her robe, Patience took the stairs rapidly. "As far away from you as possible." Once on the second floor, she stormed into their bedroom. By the time Josh got there, she already had her suitcase open.

"Wait just a minute." Josh yanked a handful of filmy lingerie from her fist and tossed it aside.

Patience gasped in protest as he laid a hand on her shoulder and hauled her back to his side.

"There is no sense in you losing your inheritance in a fit of temper," he said grimly.

"You think that's all this is, my temper?" Patience wrested herself from his grip, picked up a boot and sent it sailing at his head.

"Yes."

She followed it with another. "Well, once again you are wrong."

One minute they were standing apart, the next he was drawing her close.

He gripped her shoulders loosely. "Don't you think you should at least think about this first, before you call the whole thing off?"

Patience wiggled free. "Not in this instance, no."

Giving up without warning, he dropped back onto the bed. He sat with his back against the headboard. His feet crossed at the ankle, his hands folded casually on his washboard-flat stomach, he couldn't have looked more relaxed.

"You can't give up on us," he continued confidently.

Patience tossed back her head and gave a short, incredulous laugh. The heck she couldn't. "Why not?" she retorted feistily. "You did."

"That," Josh pointed out sternly, "was different."

I'd like to know how, Patience thought furiously as she unbelted her robe. "Right. Then only one of us knew what was really going on. Now both of us do."

"I beg to differ with you there, too." He watched with thinly veiled appreciation as she slipped off her robe and tugged on a red cotton shirt that buttoned up the front. Realizing too late that she had pulled her top on inside out, Patience stripped it off again. "Once again, you are deriding my ability to make decisions."

Josh watched as she tugged on her jeans. "When you calm down, and you will calm down, you will see things differently."

She grabbed her suitcase, the clothes falling out of it every which way, and hurried down the stairs. "Don't bet on it."

7:41

"OKAY, SO I COULDN'T LEAVE, SO sue me," Patience told Tweedles several hours later, after she had sort of slept on the sofa. She stroked her Persian cat behind her ears, watching as Tweedles's six newborn kittens nursed contentedly at their mama's side in their basket in the utility room. "I had an obligation to stay and see Trace and Cody get married. Assuming, of course, that their situations have gone better than mine. It would have been wrong of me to leave the Silver Spur before the day is out, knowing, as I do, that their nuptials are going to occur late this afternoon."

Footsteps sounded in the adjacent kitchen. Patience tensed as Josh strode in carrying a denim dress shirt, brown tweed sport jacket and tie. "Unfortunately, this is it," he announced, holding them up for her perusal.

Patience brought her knees up to her chest and sat back against the washer. Without electricity, the house seemed dead and quiet. With the exception of the occasional purring of the kittens—or snores from Goldie, Josh's retriever, who was sleeping soundly in the kitchen—there was no other noise. It would get even quieter when Josh left. But she didn't want to think about that any more than she wanted to think about the clothes he was holding in front of her.

Aware he wasn't going to go away unless she said something, Patience retorted calmly, "What do you mean, this is it?" She regarded him with exasperation. " 'It' what?"

He hung the shirt, coat and tie on the hook above the washer. "The extent of the formal clothing I own."

Patience stayed where she was, curled up into a little ball. "And your point is—?"

Still lingering in the doorway, he gave her an exasperated glance. "The wedding is in less than eight hours."

"So?" Feeling trapped in the small utility room, Patience stood and brushed by him.

"Have you given any thought to what we're going to wear?" Josh asked as she marched by, her fists clenched tightly at her sides.

Patience spun around, unable to help but rise to the bait. "You can't seriously think I am going to go through with this!"

Josh shrugged. He came toward her. Before she knew what he was up to, he had trapped her against the counter, one hand braced firmly on either side of her. "It's what Max wanted. Until you knew who I was," he emphasized softly, "it was what we both wanted."

Patience tried to step past him. To her dismay, he countered by coming even closer, until their bodies brushed seductively from chest to knee. "I never said that."

"No. You didn't." He stopped her gasp of protest with a hard, firm kiss that swiftly had her quivering from head to toe. He bent his head and nuzzled her neck, leaned against her and held her tightly. "But you showed it to me in a hundred different ways." He kissed her forehead, the tip of her nose, her mouth. "You showed it to me in the way you kissed me and touched me—"

Patience moaned and turned her head away. She had sworn to herself that she would not give in to him, but her heart was already melting, her body quickening at just the sight and smell and touch of him. "Stop it." Much more and she really would end up wrapped in his arms once again, making love to him with every fiber of her being.

He buried his face in her hair and held her close. "The truth painful, is it?"

Very, Patience thought. Because whether she wanted to admit it or not, it was going to kill her to let him go.

Hand on his chest, she shoved until he leaned back. Looking up into the ruggedly handsome contours of his face, she told him what she had already regretfully concluded. "What we have had the past forty hours, twenty-two minutes and—" she glanced at her watch "—twenty-seven seconds was sex, and a little romance, built on dishonesty. Fortunately—" she dragged in a ragged breath, doing her best to control her sky-rocketing emotions "—in the last hour or so I have recognized the error of my ways, or maybe I should say your ways—"

"How about our ways?" he cut in, a facetious twinkle in his gray eyes.

"—and come to my senses!" Patience concluded, trying hard not to appreciate his warmth and solid male presence.

He grinned drolly, apparently appreciating the flare of her temper even as he remained loath to let her go. "Well, now we know how you feel," he teased gently.

"We certainly do!" Patience fumed as her heartbeat accelerated even more.

A long moment passed as he regarded her with all the tenderness and understanding of the man he'd been, and the courage and determination of the man he'd become.

"Isn't it time we learned how I feel?" he prompted, brushing a light kiss on her forehead.

Her skin tingling, Patience admitted reluctantly, "I suppose it's only fair."

Hands on her waist, he lifted her onto the kitchen counter. "When I held you in my arms, when I sheathed my body in yours, when we very possibly made a baby, it felt like more than sex to me, it felt like the kind of love that comes only once in a lifetime," he said huskily.

Patience had felt that way, too. But she was also confused and hurt, so much so that she didn't trust herself to think rationally. She pushed him aside and jumped down, very much afraid if she rushed into anything, as Max and Josh both obviously wanted her to, she would make another heartrending mistake. "Well, you're wrong!" she said agitatedly.

He stepped back and threw his hands up in the air. "Here we go again."

Her attention caught by his scowl of displeasure, Patience stared at him in surprise. "What do you mean by that?" she asked suspiciously.

He leveled a lecturing finger her way. "I mean this was precisely what was wrong with our relationship the first time! You deciding on a stand—in this case, telling Max we were getting married on Valentine's Day no matter what anyone else thought or did—and then taking it for both of us."

As she studied his face and realized he meant what he said with all his heart, the hurt Patience felt was staggering. "You told me you wanted to get married," she protested.

"I did." His expression gentling, Josh took her in his arms again. His face was inches from hers. "But I would have been just as happy waiting a while longer. You were the one who was in the rush."

Patience turned her back to him, knowing everything he had just said was true. "Well, that's not the case now," she continued defiantly.

"And it should be." Josh came up behind her and wrapped his hands around her waist. He buried his face in her hair and spoke into her ear. "Damn it, Patience, we have the chance to be together again. We have a chance to have a baby together." Hands on her shoulders, he turned her to face him. "Hell, we may have already made a child together!" he reminded her emotionally, still holding her close. His eyes searched hers. "Doesn't that mean anything to you?"

Tears stung her eyes as she thought of all that they stood to lose if they didn't somehow find a way to work this out. "Of course it does."

"Then—?"

Swallowing hard against the ache in her throat, she pressed a hand to her heart. "Don't you think I want to be reckless, to just say the heck with common sense and do what I want to do at this very moment? But I can't, Josh," she said in a low, anguished voice. *I can't risk being hurt like that again.* She lifted her brimming eyes to his. "I'm not a crazy kid anymore. I have to act responsibly. And so do you. Getting married now... knowing who you are... what you've done in not telling me or taking me with you... Don't you understand that the way you hurt me and kept on hurting me changes everything?" Which was, she thought wearily, a part of her already jumping to his defense, exactly why he hadn't told her everything to begin with.

Josh nodded solemnly. His eyes met hers in a way that made her heart pound. He slipped his hands into her hair and, ever so tenderly, brought her face close to his. "I know you need a little time to figure things out. And I'm willing to give it to you. It's only right, after all." His lips touched hers, once, and then again. "So if you want to put off the marriage until you feel you can trust me again, I won't fight you on it. But I still can't leave without kissing you just one more time."

JOSH KNEW, even as he swept Patience into his arms and carried her up the stairs to the privacy of their bedroom, that he was taking unfair advantage. He couldn't help it. He had to have her. Had to let her know how he felt and try to change her mind. Now, while the opportunity to do so was still there. He took heart in the fact she made not a sound or gesture of protest but simply waited, her eyes wide with wonder and desire, for him to make his next move.

He set her gently down on the floor next to the bed, so she was standing once again, wrapped in the warm cradle of his arms. She let out a tremulous breath. "I should have known you were trouble the first moment I laid eyes on you again," she said, unable to completely suppress a grin as she wreathed both arms around his neck.

Josh returned her rueful smile with one of his own as he tugged the hem of her shirt from the waistband of her jeans. Clearly, as bleak as the future looked to her at that moment, as angry with him as she still was for not taking her with him into danger, there was a part of her that couldn't let go. Which meant she did not want their time to end any more than he did. He took solace in that as he unbuttoned her blouse. "Well, you know now. We both do. 'Cause you're right," he drawled softly as he parted the edge of her blouse, revealing first the lacy white camisole and soft white curves of her breasts. "I have changed. And so have you. And we're just going to have to reconcile ourselves to that." Just as they were going to have to reconcile themselves to the fact that there would never ever be anyone else for either of them.

Tears shimmered in her eyes as she reached for the buckle on his belt and the zipper of his jeans. "You're asking me to forget and forgive?"

"Just forgive, Patience," Josh corrected softly, kissing her with the reverence she deserved. "Never, ever forget. Everything that's happened has made us who we are today. Everything that's happened has led us to this chance." And it was a chance he was not going to blow. Not if he could help it.

Having finished undressing her, he lowered her to the bed. He leaned across her, bracing his arms on either side of her. Starting with her lips, he worked his way down her body, kissing and caressing every inch of her as she moaned with desire. He kissed her but could never get enough, until every taste was as potent as the last. He seduced her, taking her in his own way, his own time, a way he knew would prolong her pleasure and take her to the brink again and again and again. If they had only today, he wanted to hang on to every single moment and make it last. A lifetime if necessary.

Patience surged against Josh, as lost in the wonder of finding each other again as he was. She knew he was giving her everything and she wanted to give him everything in return. She pressed her lips against his, seeking even as she demanded, exploring even as she savored, until his body pulsed at the sound of her soft, incoherent pleas and she, too, was beyond holding back. Needing, wanting more than just a taste of paradise, she grasped his bare shoulders and guided him on top of her.

Drawn into the dazzling pleasure, he took her with him, both of them scaling the heights, coming back down again. For long, precious moments they held each other, trembling. Then, their hearts full of the precious beauty of the moment, they reached for each other and started all over again.

PATIENCE LAY ON HER SIDE, Josh's arms wrapped around her, tears of release sliding down her cheeks. She had never felt so loved as she had just now when they made love again and again in the morning light, or so scared and uncertain about the future. Their future. Was she the only one who had noticed a desperation to their kisses or had the sense they were on the very edge of losing everything, especially each other? Was this how Josh had felt all those years they had been apart? Like he could live only in that very moment? Like absolutely everything and everyone he loved might be cruelly ripped from him at any time?

Josh's arms tightened around her. "You're crying."

"A little. I can't help it." Patience turned so she was facing him. She wrapped her arms around him and buried her face in the fragrant, hair-whorled warmth of his chest. "I wanted so much for us. I still do."

His hand stroked down her hair, then came around to lift her face to his. "But you're afraid we're never going to have it? Is that it?"

Patience sat up, dragging the edge of the rumpled sheet with her. She couldn't, wouldn't, lie to him. She sat cross-legged next to him. Maybe it was time they got it all out in the open. Maybe then the fear she felt would not be so heartrendingly intense. She blotted the moisture from her face with the tips of her fingers. "Aren't you?"

He folded his hands behind his head, his gray eyes hesitant. "If you're asking me what tomorrow holds—" he began.

Patience shook her head. The promises she wanted from him were much closer to home and heart. The promises she wanted from him, she decided swiftly, would be enough. But she would have to get them first. "I want you to promise me that you'll never leave me behind again, Josh."

Regret etched harsh lines in his ruggedly handsome face. "I can't, Patience. Not if leaving you were the only way to protect you," he replied so quickly she knew he hadn't even had to think about it.

He was silent a long moment, studying her. "That's not what you wanted to hear, is it?" he asked reluctantly at last.

Patience drew a bolstering breath, her fear of losing all they had rediscovered increasing. But, like him, she wasn't willing to throw in the towel and give up just yet. She met his glance equably and insisted, "If we are going to have a future together, Josh, and I admit now that I want one, I need to know you won't make that decision for or without me, if and when the time comes that you do have to disappear again or take on a new identity."

She could tell by the grim, brooding look on his face that Josh was flashing back to the night his father had died and the oceans of regret that had tortured him since. "You don't know what you're asking of me," he said roughly. He sat up against the headboard and reached behind him to adjust the pillows.

Patience thought she did. "Or what you, Josh, are asking of me, to think that I could live otherwise," she asserted quietly as she felt her lips begin to quiver.

"Listen to me, Patience." Josh laid his hands on her shoulders firmly. "My lack of immediate action cost my father his life. Had I only asked a lot of questions a lot sooner, I would have known what he was up against, I would have been able to talk him into turning state's witness. But I didn't. And they came for him, and he died anyway.'' His hands tightened protectively on her shoulders and he hauled her against him, shifting her so that she was sitting across his lap, the sheet still wrapped around her, the pillows at his back.

He stroked her bare skin gently as he continued in a low, anguished voice, ''I couldn't bear the same thing happening to you because of me and what I did to put the men who hurt my father away.''

Briefly, Patience rested her cheek against his. ''I understand how you feel. And though the odds are against it, I understand the day may come when we'd both be in danger,'' she said pragmatically, knowing she could live with that.

''But—?'' Josh picked up on all she wasn't saying as she drew slowly away.

''If you run again, I still want to know that you'll take me with you,'' she said earnestly, swallowing hard when she saw the uncooperative look come into his gray eyes. ''Promise me, Josh,'' she persisted hoarsely. ''Please. It's the only way I'll ever have any peace of mind.''

But to her dismay, he was already shaking his head no. ''I can't,'' he repeated autocratically.

Patience thought about waking up one morning to find him gone. Never knowing whether he was dead or alive. Never knowing if she would ever see him again. And she knew she couldn't bear it. Not again. She had lost him once because he had shut her out, unfairly. She could not, would not, go through it again.

''I have to protect you, Patience.'' His jaw tensed stubbornly, letting her know that on this issue he was about as easily moved as a five-ton boulder. "And I'll do it with my life, if need be," he emphasized strongly.

Patience sighed. "Even if it costs us the chance to be together?" she asked brokenly as she felt all her dreams come crashing down around her.

Josh nodded grimly, his position unchanged. It did not matter to him that he was breaking her heart, Patience thought resentfully. He only cared about protecting her!

"Even then," he said.

1:35

"SO THIS IS WHAT YOU meant by things being in a state of emergency when I caught you on the cell phone a while ago," Cisco drawled several hours later.

Patience turned to see him striding toward her. "One of the barns was struck by lightning last night."

"Lose any of the horses?"

"No." Patience paused in the act of inspecting the damage and wiped the soot from her cheeks. "We managed to get them all out, including Mandy and her new foal, Impatience, who is doing well, by the way."

"Glad to hear it. As for the rest, you know you've got insurance on all the buildings and the equipment and livestock therein."

Tears streaming down her face, Patience nodded.

Acting out of a friendship that went back years, Cisco took Patience into his arms. "But it was still upsetting?" he guessed.

Patience clung to Cisco as she sobbed into his chest, knowing she had never needed her old friend more. "Oh, Cisco. You don't know the half of it."

1:15

"IT DIDN'T TAKE HER LONG to replace me, did it?" Josh growled a short distance away as he carefully checked over Mandy and her foal.

"Careful, boss, you're sounding jealous," Soaring Eagle said.

Relieved to find Impatience's temperature normal and her lungs clear, Josh turned to Soaring Eagle and handed over care of the newborn foal and her mama. "Should I be jealous?" Josh asked casually, wondering if Soaring Eagle knew something he didn't about Patience and Cisco, who, even now, were looking unusually close. Emotionally as well as physically.

Soaring Eagle added feed and fresh water to Mandy's stall. "Not if she agreed to marry you, as per terms of Max McKendrick's will."

"That's just it." Josh frowned. "She hasn't." Though he was still sticking to her like glue and honoring the terms stipulated in Max's will, just in case.

"Any chance she'll say yes? You've still got—" Soaring Eagle stepped outside the barn and glanced at the position of the sun for reference "—a good hour before you have to be at the wedding site."

Josh looked at his wristwatch and determined Soaring Eagle was right. "How do you know the timetable for the wedding?" he asked brusquely, feeling all the more irritable as he realized his time with Patience really was running out.

"Invitations were sent out to the hands on all the various ranch operations. So I reckon I'm going and so is everyone else."

Josh swore. That, he hadn't known. "Too bad in our case the bride and the groom aren't going," he said bitterly.

Soaring Eagle looked at Patience, who was still in Cisco's arms, and then turned back to study Josh. "Sure it isn't too late to change that?" he asked.

1:00

"FEELING BETTER?" Cisco asked Patience as he patted her gently on the back.

Patience nodded. She drew away slightly, accepting the handkerchief Cisco offered. "I'm sorry." She blotted her eyes and blew her nose. "I don't know what's come over me today. I've been acting like a complete idiot all morning." First, making love with Josh like there was no tomorrow, then finding out there really was no tomorrow with him...not one she could count on, anyway.

But more depressing, dejecting and debilitating than that was the knowledge that Josh still wouldn't take her with him...that he would still leave her behind after everything they'd been through. She had expected more from him.

"Maybe I could help," Cisco said gently, still patting her on the back.

"I don't know how," Patience sniffed, "since Josh won't even acknowledge he made a mistake." *In leaving me behind.* "Or promise he'll do things differently in the future."

Cisco tipped the brim of his hat back so it was no longer shading his eyes. "You're not making much sense," he said finally.

Nor, because of her need to protect Josh, could Patience explain so Cisco would understand everything.

Holly Diehl came up to join them unexpectedly. After briskly introducing herself to Cisco, she said, "I think I know what's bothering Patience. If you wouldn't mind, Mr. Kidd, I'd like to talk to Patience alone."

Cisco looked from one woman to another. Finally realizing it was okay with Patience, he nodded. "Sure. I have to tell Josh that, in accordance with the wishes expressed in Max's last will and testament, I left the wedding clothes for both of you up at the studio. Should you change your mind and decide to go through with the ceremony, Patience, you'll find everything you need up at the house."

Figuring if anyone could shed light on how she should handle the situation with Josh it was Holly Diehl, Patience walked with Holly over to the corral. Josh was a short distance away, talking with Slim and Soaring Eagle. Just looking at Josh, watching him, Patience was filled with yearning. "You know who I am," Holly asserted.

Patience nodded. "The FBI agent charged with Josh's protection before and after the trial."

"I wish Josh hadn't told you who he is."

Patience turned her back on Josh and leaned against the corral fence. She focused her gaze on the hired hands who were busy cleaning out the muck and smoldering ruins of the foaling barn. "I would've figured it out sooner or later."

Holly Diehl looked skeptical about that as she shoved her hands in the pockets of her jeans. "Would you? I think he's changed a great deal since you knew him."

"Not enough, apparently," Patience muttered darkly, because she was still head over heels in love with him.

"Does this mean you are not going to marry him after all?"

Patience shrugged as she studied the blazing blue sky overhead. It really was turning out to be a beautiful day. "What's the point in knowing you made a mistake if you wouldn't do it all over differently again?" And Josh, darn his stubborn soul, wasn't about to do anything differently, Patience thought bitterly.

"So he told you he would run again, if it came to that," Holly guessed.

Patience's lips curled sardonically as she recalled Josh's hopelessly protective attitude. "He is determined to protect me, even if it means leaving me again without so much as a word or kiss goodbye."

"Josh may or may not have told you, but I was around last night during the storm. I wasn't sure how this thing with you was going to play out, and I wanted to be around in case Josh needed me. We at the agency owe him a lot. My colleagues and I would like him to be happy. We'd like him to be able to stay here, where he is safe."

The truth be told, so would she, Patience thought. "What is your point?" she asked irritably.

"I didn't see you thinking of yourself first last night during the fire. You went straight to the barn that housed all those foals and helped Josh and the men get them out of there, regardless of the danger to yourself."

"That was different." Patience squared her shoulders defiantly. "The mares and their foals needed my protecting. None of them had experience dealing with fire, and that was a completely terrifying, utterly un-expected occurrence.''

''Still, you could have darted in, opened all the stall doors and simply left the animals to fend for them-selves.''

''And what if the mares and their foals hadn't fig-ured out what to do?'' Patience shot back. ''If we had lost any of our foals or our mares in the fire, I never would have forgiven myself.''

''Perhaps that's what Josh feels now toward you, in-tensified a hundred million times,'' Holly Diehl re-torted meaningfully.

Patience fell silent, thinking about that.

''For the record,'' Soaring Eagle said as he walked past them, leading one of the ranch stallions, ''the rest of the hired hands and I think you should give Josh a second chance, too. To make up for whatever he's done to tick you off, Patience.''

Patience sighed. She gave Soaring Eagle a look that let him know she did not appreciate his advice.

''Funny, Soaring Eagle doesn't seem the type to horn in on someone else's conversation,'' Holly mused, in-clining her head at the trainer after he had passed.

Frowning, Patience dug the toe of her boot in the mud. ''He's not. Normally, that is.''

''Then he must want you and Josh together a lot.''

Patience shrugged. ''He's always had a protective attitude toward me, too. All the hired hands have, since most of them watched me grow up.''

''Nevertheless, Soaring Eagle must think Josh is good for you.''

''So do a lot of people, including my dear departed Uncle Max. It doesn't mean any of them are right.'' Patience sighed.

"It doesn't mean they're wrong, either." Holly touched her arm encouragingly. "Take a chance, Patience. Enjoy the moment. After all, what have you got to lose that you haven't already lost? And survived."

00:50

CISCO INTERCEPTED JOSH, just as he came out of the foaling barn. "I left your tux up at the house, Josh."

Josh paused, taking in the fact that Patience was still deep in conversation with Holly Diehl over by the corral fence. He had explained to Holly that Patience was no threat to his new identity and asked Holly to put in a good word for him in the hopes they might still be able to work things out. Judging from the looks on their faces, it did not appear his strategy to win Patience's hand in marriage was working. Which meant not only were they letting Max down, they were letting themselves down, too. "Did you also bring Patience a wedding gown?" he asked Cisco, trying not to sound dejected.

Cisco nodded. "It's with the tux."

"And Patience knows this?" Josh asked with a disgruntled sigh.

"I told her just a moment ago," Cisco confirmed.

Yet Patience was still talking with Holly over by the fence. "Then you must also know there isn't going to be any wedding," Josh said.

Cisco shrugged. "I know she's having last-minute jitters."

"What she feels is a hell of a lot more than simple prewedding jitters," Josh interrupted.

Cisco stared at Josh pointedly. "I know she's upset."

"Enough to find solace in your arms." *Instead of mine.*

Cisco paused, but to Josh's disappointment, he didn't rise to the bait that would have, Josh was sure, led to a fistfight between the two of them. "Is there some reason she shouldn't marry you?" Cisco asked Josh matter-of-factly.

Actually, Josh thought, there were plenty, the least being that he could not, no matter how desperately he wanted to do so, promise Patience that their life would run smoothly from this point forward. "Isn't there always?" Josh retorted casually at last.

Cisco frowned. "I admit I've known Patience a long time. I've never seen her the way she is around you."

"And what is that?" Josh mocked, furious to find Cisco being so damn civil to him at long last. "Highly agitated and upset?"

"In love."

Josh swallowed. He was almost afraid to hope for a happy outcome here. Up until now, his life hadn't exactly been brimming over with bliss. "She tell you that?"

"Not in so many words."

Josh grimaced. "Just as I thought."

"Look, I know Patience. Regardless of what she's said to you this morning, or last night, or whenever, she wants things to work out for you two," Cisco insisted.

So did he. The road to hell was paved with good intentions. "That's the problem," Josh said gruffly. "Despite our best intentions, things don't always work out."

"But they could," Cisco insisted with lawyerly calm, "if you were willing to meet her halfway on whatever this mysterious issue is that is pulling the two of you apart.''

To do that meant promising he might have to put Patience in the kind of danger that could cost her her life. And though Josh was willing to risk it for himself, he wasn't willing to risk it for her. He loved her too much for that. Surely when Patience thought about it, she would see that. ''I can't.''

''Then you're a fool,'' Cisco said, exasperated.

''Maybe,'' Josh allowed.

''And that being the case, I suggest you either wise up fast—before you blow the chance of a lifetime—or forget the marriage Max wanted for you two and clear the hell out, now, before you hurt Patience any more than you already have. Because if you turn Patience down in such a public way, knowing she has already been publicly humiliated and left at the altar once, there is going to be no way she'll ever forgive you for this.''

Chapter Thirteen

Dear Patience,
I am not sure what to do. To reconcile with my fiancé, I'd have to eat crow.

Sincerely,
Proud In Pecos

Dear Proud in Pecos,
Pass the salt and pepper, please. Choose your pride or your love.

Thinkin' It's No Contest,
Patience

00:29

"Stop looking at me like that, Goldie," Josh told his golden retriever as he reluctantly carried a packed bag to the front door and went back for the plaid cedar cushion Goldie slept on. "You know as well as I do we have to move on again."

Goldie let out a bark and ran after him. Snatching the cedar cushion in her jaws, she tugged it back to its place beside the fireplace. Setting it down there, she plopped on top of it.

Josh released a heartfelt sigh of exasperation. "You're going to want that cushion when we get to wherever it is we're going," he warned.

Goldie wouldn't budge.

"Fine." Josh picked up his suitcase. His expression all business, he inclined his head toward the door. "C'mon then. We'll just have to leave without it."

Goldie's ears lowered in the way they always did when she was depressed. She put her head down on her paws and regarded him mournfully. Josh hated to admit it, but Goldie was displaying his feelings exactly.

Nevertheless, he thought with a heavy heart, he had a job to do, and it was an important one. He had to prevent Patience from getting hurt even more, even if it meant he was annihilated in the process. "Goldie, c'mon. Let's go." Josh followed his firm words with a whistled command.

To no avail. Goldie just lay there.

Josh dropped his bag and went back to Goldie's side. He knelt next to the retriever who had been his only steady companion and confidante for years now. Because they were of similar heart, it seemed only right that Goldie would attach herself to Patience, too. "What are you trying to tell me, Goldie?" Josh asked gently, stroking the underside of her jaw. "That I shouldn't leave? You know as well as I do that it's the only way to protect Patience. It'd be wrong to take her with me. She deserves to be safe."

Goldie lifted her head and let out a soft whine.

Josh's throat grew tight as he realized what Goldie was trying to tell him. "Yes, Goldie, I know Patience is miserable now. That's no doubt why she rushed in here and locked herself in the bedroom for the last hour or so. But she'll eventually find someone else. And hell, even if she doesn't, she'll still be better off."

Goldie let out another sharp bark.

Josh nodded, letting his canine pal know he was listening. "You're right, Goldie. There's still the problem of Patience's inheritance. I know how much Max wanted her to have part of this ranch for herself and her children. And on a practical note, she does need someone to run it for her, and a veterinarian on the premises."

Goldie whined her agreement and licked Josh's hand before looking up at him with dark, pleading eyes.

Knowing it was what he wanted, too, Josh capitulated without further argument. "Maybe you and Cisco are right. Maybe I should hang around for the wedding."

Goldie's tail thumped happily as Josh continued, "Maybe I should exchange I do's with Patience and let her save face in front of all her family and friends. Then later it can be said she found out I was a louse and she kicked me out. That'll make her look good and me look bad."

While Goldie watched attentively, Josh stood and glanced at the stairs. "So what do you think? Is there still time for me to change into my tux and pull this off?"

00:25

THE CATHEDRAL TRAIN of her old-fashioned white satin dress flowing behind her, Patience rushed out of the bedroom and ran smack-dab into a hard male chest covered by a dove gray coat and starched white shirt.

"You're dressed," Patience and Josh said to each other in unison.

Patience touched the cap that held the veil on her head and took a deep breath. Josh had never looked handsomer. She had never been so glad to see him.

True, they hadn't really been apart all morning. They'd been under the same roof or outside within eyesight of each other, but it seemed as if it had been ages since they had talked. Even longer since they had kissed or touched.

Was that about to change? To her disappointment, his impassive expression gave no clue.

"Seems we have a wedding to go to," Patience said after a moment.

Josh motioned for her to go first. "Seems that way, yes."

Patience swept down the stairs ahead of him. "I'm glad you came to your senses."

He joined her at the foot of the stairs. "I'm glad you came to yours." He looked her up and down in an approving manner. "I know it's been a rough couple of days for you, Patience—"

"For us both," she agreed softly.

"But you'll feel better once you inherit," Josh soothed.

Patience quirked a brow. He was making this sound awfully one-sided. "And you won't?"

"I'm leaving it all to you."

"I see." Patience gritted her teeth and folded her arms in front of her. She glowered up at him as she inhaled the bracing scent of his after-shave. "I've written letters to readers about men like you," she stated obstinately.

He quirked a brow, intrigued. "Men like me being men who—?" His gray eyes still fastened on hers, he left the thought hanging.

She spun away from him. "Have one foot—or in your case, both feet—out the door from the start." She headed to the kitchen to check on Tweedles and her kittens. They were still in their basket in the utility room and doing fine, to her relief. Goldie had dragged her cushion in and was lying next to them, her head on her paws, peacefully watching over them all.

Leery of disturbing them, Patience tiptoed back out and into the living room, Josh hard on her heels.

"Is that what you think?" Josh cornered her next to the bookcase. "That I don't *want* to marry you?"

Patience backed up until she touched wood and tilted her chin at him. Their eyes clashed and held. She drew a breath at the dangerous glimmer in his gray eyes. "I think you have always been afraid of marriage to me, yes. As a matter of fact, I think you'll look for any and every excuse not to—"

Josh interrupted her with a hard, swift kiss. Ignoring her gasp of dismay, he braced an arm on either side of her, leaned in close and deepened it even more.

Sensations swept through her, more potent than before. Though Patience had sworn she would not give in to him again until he did things her way, she found herself responding anyway. Only when she was limp in his arms, her mouth softening unmistakably beneath his, did he lift his lips from hers.

Shaken by the ruthless display of passion that had and always would exist between them, Patience stared up at him. "What was that about?" she whispered finally, still tingling from the top of her head to her toes with the impact of their fiery embrace.

"I don't know," Josh drawled, stroking a hand gently down her face and looking deep into her eyes. He grinned and continued with the swaggering confidence all the McKendricks and their partners seemed to have. "It just felt right. Kind of like my staying on is beginning to feel right."

Patience sucked in a breath, almost afraid to hope. Unable not to. "If you chose to do that—" she began, knowing this was her chance to make amends, too. To come out of this with the happy heart and full life Max had wanted her to have. And a baby, too. A baby that belonged to her and Josh.

"Yes?"

She curled her fingers around the lapels of his dove gray coat. "I wouldn't ask you to promise me anything, Josh." She looked into his face, her heart pounding. As she continued softly, persuasively, her voice brimmed with all that was in her heart. "I know we can't predict the future. And I understand now—you wanting to protect me."

Josh's eyes darkened with relief as he clasped her to him and waited for her to go on.

Swallowing around the lump in her throat, Patience did. "So, after reconsidering, I have decided I won't insist you take me with you, should the time ever arrive when you might have to leave."

Josh went very still. So still she thought she might have lost everything.

"What if I want to take you with me?" he asked quietly, searching her eyes. "What then?"

Patience didn't even have to think about it. "Then I'd go. No questions asked. No argument given," she said simply, knowing she trusted him and his love and concern for her that much. He'd been talking about taking her with him this time! She paused, her heart pounding as his words sank in. "Does that mean—?"

"Yes." He bent to kiss her. As she returned the lingering caress, joy bubbled up inside her, almost overwhelming in its intensity.

Finally, trembling, they broke apart. The moment they did, she had to ask. "Josh?"

"Hmm?" He brushed the moisture from her lip with the pad of his thumb, and she did the same for him.

"What changed your mind?" Patience asked.

Josh quirked an eyebrow, his gentle gaze never leaving her face. "Besides the fact that Goldie flat out refused to leave?" he teased.

Patience nodded. "Besides that."

Josh wrapped his arms around her and gathered her close. "I realized that my deep need to protect you came from the fact that I love you more than life. And that without you, I have no life. And," he said, his voice catching slightly, "I realized that if you felt even half of what I do—"

"For the record," Patience interrupted with a smile, "it's equal to, if not more."

"Then we really have no choice but to stick by each other, through thick and thin."

"On the run, or home on the Silver Spur," Patience concurred.

Josh kissed her again, then, still holding tight, drew back to warn, "I'll always be looking over my shoulder, Patience."

She knew. "Then I'll be looking over with you," she promised calmly. "The important thing is that we love each other."

"And we do," he said firmly as happiness surged back into his eyes, "love each other deeply."

Patience smiled, knowing all was right with their world at long last. "Yes," she said softly, standing on tiptoe to kiss him once again. "We do."

00:15

READY TO HEAD OUT, Josh and Patience opened the door and found Soaring Eagle standing on the other side. He was grinning from ear to ear. "Cisco Kidd bet me you two would come to your senses, and just in the nick of time. He was right."

Josh nodded at the horse saddled and waiting, a magnificent white stallion. It was bedecked in silver wedding finery. "What's this all about?" he asked, clearly as surprised as Patience.

Soaring Eagle smiled and elaborated. "Max felt you two should ride to the wedding site in the most romantic style possible."

"Then we won't disappoint." Josh lifted Patience up into the saddle and climbed on after her.

Patience arranged the skirts of her wedding gown and cuddled against him. "At last we have everything we've ever dreamed of. The question is," she said worriedly as they took off, "have things worked out as happily for my siblings, too?"

Josh tightened his arms around her waist. "There's only one way to find out."

00:00:56

AS THEY ARRIVED at the wedding site, Pearl came out to greet them. She was followed by Patience's brother Cody—who to Patience's surprise and delight had shaved off his beard!—and his bride-to-be, Callie

Sheridan. Both looked as deliriously happy as she and Josh were, Patience was pleased to note. In fact, Cody looked a damn sight more civilized than when she had last seen him. But where were the other two in the triple wedding party?

"Where's Trace and Susannah?" Patience asked as Josh dismounted and, capable hands on her waist, swung her down from the saddle, too.

"We don't know," Cody said, looking worried.

"None of us have heard from him or Susannah or any of their kids for hours now," his bride-to-be, Callie, added. Like Patience, she was dressed in a beautiful white wedding gown. Cody was wearing a tux. "And considering the storm we had last night, we can't help but wonder if they are all right," Cody said grimly.

"Never mind if they'll make the wedding on time," Pearl worried.

Patience glanced at her watch. This was not like Trace. He was always punctual to a fault. Early, even. Susannah, though not as rule-driven as her brother Trace, was equally responsible. Which made this turn of events even stranger. With just seconds left to go until the deadline set by their Uncle Max, Patience wondered anxiously, what could be keeping Susannah and Trace?

He's at home in denim; she's bathed in diamonds...
Her tastes run to peanut butter; his to pâté...
They're bound to be together

for
Richer,
for
Poorer

We're delighted to bring you more of the kinds of stories
you love in FOR RICHER, FOR POORER—where lovers
are drawn by passion...but separated by price!

In June watch for:

#634 *REBEL WITH A CAUSE*
By Kim Hansen

Don't miss any of the
FOR RICHER, FOR POORER
books—only from

AMERICAN ◆ ROMANCE®

MILLION DOLLAR SWEEPSTAKES

If you are looking for more titles by

CATHY GILLEN THACKER

Don't miss these fabulous stories by one of
Harlequin's most renowned authors:

Harlequin American Romance®

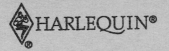

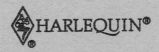